HUSTLE2HARD
PUBLICATIONS PRESENTS

Riding Dirty

*How far will you ride for
your nigga?*

By

Shoney K

This book is dedicated to the three special D's in
my life
Darren, Destiny, DJ

2016 has not been a good year for my city. Hearts are hurting over the senseless killings. Chicago let's put the guns down and uplift one another...

R.I.P Telly

R.I.P Heavy

R.I.P. Sloppy

Continue to rest peacefully Danielle, you are truly missed

PROLOGUE

My baby…my baby…who in the hell shot my baby!" Yvette yelled out in pain as if she were the one shot. Yvette stood about three inches from her daughter's body. She stared at Jazzy as she lay helplessly in the hospital bed with all type of tubes running from her body. Yvette knew that Jazzy lived a fast life, but she never expected to see her daughter laid up in a hospital bed from several bullets, fighting for her life. Only if she could turn back the hand of times, she would have been more active in her daughter's life after Jazzy's father's death.

"Ma'am, I'm Doctor Campbell," the short, fat, grey-eyed African American doctor spoke in the sincerest voice as she entered the room. She approached Yvette and rested her hand on Yvette's shoulder. "Can you please have a seat while I brief you on your daughter's condition?"

Through her pain and tears Yvette said, "Doc, all I want to know is, if my baby is going to be alright? Is my baby going to live? She's only twenty-two and she has her whole life ahead of her. Please tell me that she is going to make it."

The expression on Doctor Campbell's face told it all. Yvette knew the news she was about to hear wasn't going to be good. Her tears fell at an extremely fast pace down her face. There was no stopping them; no matter how hard she tried. The only thing that could stop her tears from falling was if Jazzy jumped out of that bed and said, "Momma, no need to cry. I'm alright" but from the looks of it, that would never happen.

"Before you say anything, can you please drop to your knees with me while I talk to God? Let's pray," Yvette asked the doctor.

Doctor Campbell wasn't against it at all. She had seen so many mothers cry a river over their child as they fought for their life. What the doctor was witnessing wasn't new to her. She sees death every day. Death knocks at the hospital door at least five times a day as a result of gunplay. It's a shame that society has come to this.

"Yes, I will pray with you."

Doctor Campbell put her clipboard down on a chair and then she and Yvette dropped to their knees on the side of Jazzy's bed and rested their elbows against it.

Yvette spoke through tears that she didn't believe would ever stop falling from her eyes.

"God, please don't take my baby away from me; she's all I got. I know I haven't been the best mother in the world, but don't punish me like this. Give me another chance to prove to you and her that I can be a great mother. If you let her live, I promise to take her away from this horrible life that she has been accustomed to. Please cover her in Your blood. I need her, God. I need her with me. There is no me without her. Heal her body and spirit so she can pull through this. God, I refused to bury my baby. I'm not supposed to bury my baby; my baby is supposed to bury me. Don't let her die. Please, don't let her die. I need my baby. I need my baby. I need my baby!" She repeated those words over and over again until she felt Doctor Campbell's arms embrace her.

Doctor Campbell helped Yvette off her knees and led her to a chair. "It's time I brief you on your daughter's condition," she said as she picked up the clip board."

This is the part that Doctor Campbell hated most about her job. She hated to see parents in pain. There was no good way to break bad news; but it had to be done.

Doctor Campbell began to speak, "Jasmine was shot three times with a 40 caliber handgun."

"Oh Lord," Yvette shouted as she held her hand up to her chest, but Doctor Campbell continued delivering the news of Jazzy's condition.

"She was shot once in her chest and once in the left leg."

Doctor Campbell paused for a minute because she knew what she was about to say next was going to break Yvette down even more than what she already was.

"The last bullet hit her in her mid-section and lodged into her spinal cord. The bullet left her paralyzed from the waist down and it also damaged her liver and kidney. The bullet to her chest caused a lot of damage as well, but Jasmine is a fighter because if she weren't, with the wounds she has sustained, she wouldn't be here. Keep in mind we are not out of harm's way just yet, but the point that this 135 pound girl is still here with us after seven hours of surgery, shows me that she will pull through.

After listening to what Doctor Campbell had to say, Yvette's did a 360. It was like she was a new person. She wiped her tears away, "There has to be some type of mistake. You all need to go back and re-run those motherfuckin' tests. My daughter is not paralyzed! I will not accept that shit for nothing in the world. You must have her chart mixed up with somebody else," Yvette was stern while speaking; the weak, vulnerable side of her had disappeared.

"I know this is hard for you to accept, but Jazzy will never walk again." Doctor Campbell rested her hand on Yvette's shoulder again trying to give her a bit of comfort.

"Bitch, don't touch me!" Yvette shouted as she pushed Doctor Campbell's hand away.

"You say you a doctor; right?" Not waiting for an answer she kept talking, "Then fixed my damn baby!"

"We have done everything that we can do."

"See, that's what wrong with you doctors. Y'all don't try hard enough!"

"I understand your frustration. Just calm down please." Doctor Campbell didn't take any offense to what Yvette said. Her reaction was normal for a parent that had a child in such a condition.

Yvette broke down again. She couldn't take it. Her tears began to fall down her oval-shaped face with a vengeance. "Oh, Lord…not my baby! Whyyy," she yelled out questioning God as she dropped back down to her knees. Questioning God was something that she had never thought about doing in her life, but when pain hit so close to home, it always a different story.

Doctor Campbell continued to talk. "Jasmine is heavily sedated; she is in very little pain. We are giving her lots of pain killers through this IV," she said as she pointed at Jazzy's arm.

Yvette was at a loss for words. Her only child -- her baby -- was going to be paralyzed for the rest of her life. Yvette finally got up off the floor and took a seat right next to her daughter's bed. She rubbed her hand through her daughter's hair and then began to speak. "Baby, mommy is here for you. I'm not going anywhere. The motherfucker that did this to you will pay with their life."

On that note, Doctor Campbell left Yvette to be with her daughter. Yvette sat and talked to Jazzy as if she were wide-awake. "Where are you friends now? They should be here. This is when you need them most. I called Ferrari, baby; but I didn't get an answer. I called Sharae, Tanya and I also called Ferrari's s best friend Cornbread. What is going on? Why aren't they here with you?"

CHAPTER ONE

The Beginning

Jazzy looked through the blinds as she waited for Ferrari to pull up. She was fully dressed and ready to hit the door once he arrived. Her lightweight jacket rested on the armrest of her couch while her feet sweated a little in her Fendi rain boots. The rain was coming down extremely hard on this spring night.

"Where is this nigga," she recited while she continued to stare out the window.

Something wasn't right and she felt it in the pit of her stomach. She began to bite her fingernails because her nerves were getting the best of her. Ferrari was supposed to be at the crib at least thirty minutes ago. She had called his phone back to back, but didn't get an answer. She didn't have the slightest clue as to where he could be. When it came to business, he never missed a beat. He was always on time.

Jazzy's eyes continued to stare out the window. The rain came down harder and harder by the second and tree branches hit the windows as the wind blew forcefully. This weather wasn't good for Ferrari to be driving in; hell, it wasn't good for anybody to be driving in. A chill went through her body as her mind drifted to another place. Maybe he was in a car accident, she thought. Just as fast as that thought crossed her mind, it was erased when she saw a car pulling around the corner. She saw headlights and her heart brighten up; but when she noticed it wasn't Ferrari's car cruising up the street, her heart sadden again. Jazzy felt like a sad puppy staring out the window waiting on its master as she tried to be patient waiting for her man to arrive. She reached in her back pocket, grabbed her phone, and called Ferrari again. This time his phone went straight to voicemail. Something definitely wasn't right. She walked from the window, sat on her all-white leather couch, and searched through her call log. She searched it until she came across Cornbread's number, who was Ferrari's best friend.

She pressed the button to call his number then she placed it on speaker. "Cornbread, is Ferrari with you?" Jazzy asked after he answered his phone on the second ring.

"Naw, I'm waiting on that nigga to come through. I've been waiting for him for the last hour. He was supposed to pick me up and after he picked me up, we were headed to you so we could handle this business. I've called his phone several times, but I didn't get an answer."

"Same thing has been happening to me and now the phone is going straight to voicemail. Maybe he's in jail," Jazzy suggested with a blank look on her face. She loved Ferrari with all her heart, but she had promised herself that she would never do another bid with another nigga. The last man she was with had a three-year sentence and as soon as he came home, he left her. From that experience alone, Jazzy promised herself she couldn't be there for any man like that so she prayed that Ferrari wasn't in jail. She really wanted to spend the rest of her life with him, but doing his time with him was out of the question.

"Nigga don't have any warrants, he doesn't ride around with drugs, and he has a license and insurance. That nigga ain't in jail; trust me, baby sis."

Cornbread shouldn't have opened his mouth. He should have let her think that maybe Ferrari was in jail.

"Where is he then, Cornbread," she said sobbing. "The last time I had this gut feeling, he was in the alley in the front seat of his car with a couple of bullets in his body!"

"Jazzy, stop crying! Let me make some phone calls to see if anybody had seen him riding through the hood. I'm sure he's just tied up somewhere. You know your man always working on a get-rich-money plan."

No matter what Cornbread said to try to make the situation better, Jazzy still had a gut feeling that something wasn't right. She heard a click in her ear, indicating that she had an incoming call. She told Cornbread she had another call trying to get through and not to hang up. She took the phone from her ear and looked at it quickly. Her lips parted ways; leaving a smile on her face when she noticed it was her man -- her boo, her heart -- on the other end trying to get through. She screamed out, "It's him; it's Ferrari calling! I'll hit you right back."

Cornbread hung up the phone and Ferrari call was instantly on the line. "Baby, where in the hell are you?" Waiting for a response she never got, she said again. "Baby…baby," she repeated into the phone, but still didn't get a reply. She took the phone from her ear and looked at the screen only to see the screensaver of her and Ferrari kissing. Jazzy went to his name in her recent call log, tapped it and the phone began to ring. She put the phone back up to her ear and waited patiently as the phone rung once, twice, and on the third time an unfamiliar voice picked up.

"Hello," the voice said.

"Who the fuck is this? Where is my man?" Jazzy was heated. She immediately snapped when she heard the female voice coming from the other end of the phone.

"No need to get nasty. Calm down, baby girl. He's right here with his fine caramel ass."

Ferrari was one of them pretty boys, but not the light skin kind. He stood a good 6'4", bald fade, with dark brown eyes and his body was meticulously on point. There wasn't a fat cell on his body; all muscle. His nose was slightly long, yet it was crooked, as if it has been broke a time or two, but that didn't take away his handsomeness.

Jazzy was taken aback when she heard the female voice on the other end of her man's phone line. She knew in the back of her mind that Ferrari was cheating; but as long as she didn't see it – firsthand with her own eyes – and as long as he kept his hoes in their place, she went with the flow. Treat her good and she would treat you better;

15

make her feel like the one and only and you will be the only one. She never thought this day would come that another female would be calling her phone; especially from his number."

"Girl, I don't have time for these games you're playing. Put Ferrari on the phone. My beef isn't with you, it's with him. He's the one I'm fucking, not you. Just give him the phone so I can tell him what I need to tell him and then you two can live happily ever after.

The chick on the other end of the phone began to laugh. She laughed so hard that Jazzy became aggravated. Jazzy wanted to reach through the phone and choke the shit out of her. She hated feeling disrespected and that's exactly how she was feeling at that moment.

"Is that what you think? This nigga here don't have enough money to even smell this pussy. I'm not fucking your man li'l mamma. This shit is deeper than that. I know you don't have beef with me and you shouldn't, but because you're Ferrari's woman, I have beef with you. Your man needs you like he never needed you before."

"What the fuck are you talking about?" Jazzy had a confused look on her face. She was now pacing her living room floor.

"No need to pace the floor. You can sit back down."

Jazzy paused in her steps. *How in the hell does this bitch know I'm pacing the floor? I don't have on heels so I'm not making any noise as I walk on the hardwood floor,* Jazzy thought to herself.

"Bitch, what did you say," Jazzy asked in a voice of uncertainty even though she heard exactly what the girl had said; she just wanted the girl to repeat herself.

"You heard me correctly. If your blinds were closed, maybe it wouldn't be so easy to look inside your crib."

Jazzy walked over to the window. She noticed an all-black Buick Lacrosse with tinted windows parked across the street from her house. She closed her blinds immediately. She ran over to her purse that was positioned on her La-Z-Boy, reached in it, grabbed her other cell phone and sent Cornbread a text. She texted him three simple words, "Get here now." Jazzy didn't know what the hell this chick wanted, but anytime a female was outside of her crib, calling her from her man's phone and that female wasn't fucking him, a motherfucker had to be up to no good.

"Walk back to the window, I need to show you something," the chick said with authority.

Jazzy did what was asked of her. When she looked out the window, the girl was standing outside her car with an umbrella held over her head. She was dressed in an all-black leather bodysuit with a baseball cap on. Her Charlie Baltimore bright red hair flowed long down her back. Jazzy couldn't make out exactly what the girl looked like because of the rain and how low the baseball cap was sitting on her head.

"I'm looking…now what?" Jazzy uttered.

Jazzy's mind was still puzzled because this chick had called her from Ferrari's phone. She was also thrown off when the woman said, "Your man needs you like he never needed you before." Jazzy didn't have the slightest clue as to what was going on. She squinted her eyes a bit when she saw another body emerge from the car. She couldn't really make out who it was by the face, but the structure of the body told her it was Ferrari. His mouth was ducked taped shut and there was a rope tied around his hands so he couldn't try anything tricky. After giving Jazzy a view of her man, the woman and Ferrari got back in the car.

"Baby girl, I need you to listen to me and listen carefully. This isn't a joke and if you take it as one, your man will end up dead. Your man fucked up a lot of money, and my partner and I need our shit. If we don't get our money, I can't eat and I don't like starving. Your man owes us $200,000. I know you asking yourself how in the hell are you going to come up with that type of money, but I have a solution to your problem. It's either my way or the hard way; but you look like a smart girl so I'm sure you will make the right decision. Either way, my partner and I need our shit."

"I'm listening," Jazzy said. She was a down ass chick when it came to her man. The only thing she was against doing was jail time with him. As long as he was in the streets, she was going to ride for her nigga.

"Tomorrow morning, I will give you a call with the location and time so I can meet up with you. There are a couple of things that need to be discussed. Everything that will be asked of you needs to be accomplished within a month. No matter what I ask of you, it has to be done. The $200,000 that he owes doesn't all have to be paid monetarily. There will be certain tasks that are asked of you and that will help settle some of his debt. Do you understand?"

"I guess I have no choice, but to understand because you got my man," Jazzy barked sarcastically. "And can I speak to Ferrari? I need to know that he's alright before I do anything."

The chick giggled at Jazzy's sarcasm. "I don't see why not, but before I let you speak to him, just know tomorrow starts the clock. So the minute you wake up, be prepared to get your hands dirty."

Before the chick put Ferrari on the phone, she spoke in his ear, but loud enough so that Jazzy could hear her, "If you say anything out of pocket, I'm going to kill you and then I'm going to kill that pretty little bitch of yours."

She then snatched the duck-tape from Ferrari's mouth and held the phone up to his ear. Ferrari looked at the chick with so much hate in his eyes. He knew what this kidnapping was all about and he knew the person he was dealing with wasn't playing any games. Ferrari kept his words simple when he spoke to Jazzy.

"Baby, I'm alright. Just do what is asked of you and I will be back home safely in no time."

The only words that escaped Jazzy's mouth were, "I love you."

CHAPTER TWO

By the content of Jazzy's text, Cornbread knew that the text had to do with Ferrari. He hoped his boy was alright. He stopped everything he was doing, grabbed his .357 magnum, and then headed straight out the door to his car, straight to Jazzy's crib. The rain had finally slowed down, but the streets were still extremely wet. For the first couple of blocks, Cornbread did the speed limit, but when he thought of his boy being in trouble, he added more gas to the pedal. He drove down the street doing at least sixty miles per hour in a thirty mile per hour speed zone. Cornbread lost control of the wheel for a brief moment, almost sliding into a parked car due to the wet pavement so he reduced his speed down to forty-five. Ferrari was like a brother to Cornbread and if anything happened to him, motherfuckers would pay with more than their life.

Cornbread and Ferrari have been friends for over ten years. They met each other in the juvenile center. They both were in there for breaking and entering. They linked up one day when three dudes were jumping Cornbread in the rec room. He was no match for the three niggas. At the time, Cornbread was tall and frail. He only weighted about a hundred and fifty pounds, but times had definitely changed since then. Let's just say the ladies have a lot to hold on to now when they lay next to him. From his round belly to his thick arms and legs, Cornbread definitely keeping the ladies warm at night.

Ferrari felt like he would be less of a man if he just sat around and let the three niggas jump on Cornbread that day. He wasn't a pussy like the other niggas that stood around and watched the fight so he stepped in; not caring if he knew Cornbread or not. After that, they clicked instantly and ever since Ferrari came to Cornbread's rescue, they had formed a special bond.

After twenty-five minutes of driving, Cornbread pulled up behind Jazzy's car in the driveway. He checked his surroundings before he got out the car. Nothing seemed like it was out of the ordinary so he exited the car and used his key for entry into Jazzy's crib. Cornbread was really like family to Ferrari, that's why Ferrari didn't mind him having keys to the crib that he shared with Jazzy. The trust amongst those two was unbelievable.

"What up, baby sis," Cornbread said as soon as he walked in the house. He saw Jazzy siting on the couch, deep in thought, with her gun resting alongside her. She had her game face on. She was ready to go to war. All she cared about was getting her man back in one piece.

Don't get it twisted. Jazzy was a fuckin' lady, but she was raised to protect her family by any means necessary. Ferrari was her family and no matter what she had to do to get him home, she was going to do it. Her mind was set to kick ass and ask questions later.

A lot of people didn't take Jazzy seriously because of her baby voice, pretty face, and petite body frame. She put you in the mindset of Lil Kim, but she was just a tad bit lighter and had a smaller ass. People didn't think she could harm a fly. She had proven many wrong back in her day. Being raise in a single-family, dysfunctional home made her a tough person. It actually turned her into somebody that she didn't want to be, but she embraced herself and lived with her demons every single day.

Within her dysfunctional home came drugs, drinking and abuse; all that came on the accountability of her daddy, Jake. Jazzy took plenty of ass beatings from her dad for no apparent reason and so did her mom. One day, Jazzy walked in the house and saw her dad on top of her mom beating her as if she was a man.

"Please stop, daddy!" Jazzy yelled out, but her daddy didn't pay her any attention. He just kept beating her mother until she turned purple in the face. It didn't take much for that though, because she was a red bone. Jazzy yelled out again, "Daddy, please stop; leave mommy alone!"

"Shut up, li'l bitch," he said to his daughter. Being called a bitch by her daddy hurt more than him beating her for no apparent reason.

As her daddy continued to beat her mom, Jazzy walked away with tears rolling down her young, innocent face. She went in her mother's room and walked straight to the back of her closet. She found the shoe box where her daddy kept his gun. At the age of twelve, Jazzy knew the basics about guns. Her daddy had taught her. He taught her how to take the safety off and all she had to do next was aim and shoot. Jazzy grabbed the gun then headed back into the living room where her daddy lay on top of her mom, still beating her.

"Daddy, please stop. Stop it now," her little voice cried out.

"You're just like your damn mother, y'all don't fuckin' listen," he stopped beating Yvette for a couple of seconds and turned and looked at his daughter, "Didn't I just tell you to shut the fuck up? When I get through beating her, I'm going to beat your ass for not listening."

Jazzy could smell the liquor on his breath and she knew he was high by the look in his eyes. He couldn't do one without the other. She didn't say another word. She watched as her daddy turned back around. She took the gun from behind her back, aimed, closed her eyes, then shot. She did exactly what her daddy had taught her. The first bullet startled him when the shot went off. It went flying pass him and into the wall. It caused him to jump off her mother. When he turned around to see where the bullet had come from, he was shocked. Jazzy was the last person he expected to see holding a gun and trying to take his life.

"Put the gun down, baby," her daddy said.

Jazzy didn't pay him any attention. She knew what the outcome would be if she put the gun down. She just stood there in a daze as she continued to hold the gun.

Her daddy repeated the same words, "Put the gun down, baby," but this time, he began to walk toward her as he reached his hand out toward the gun. Yvette didn't say a word as the course of events transpired. She just laid on the floor just as shocked as any parent would be in her situation.

Scared for her life and for her mother's life, Jazzy closed her eyes again, aimed and then shot, this time hitting her target.

The bullet hit him right in the chest. Her daddy stumbled a little and then fell backwards on top of her mother. Yvette pushed him off her, jumped up, and ran to her daughter. She took the gun from Jazzy's hand as she stood there shaking uncontrollably.

"Baby, this never happened. I'm going to have somebody take care of this," Yvette grabbed Jazzy by her face, "Always protect your family by any means necessary. You did what you had to do. Let's forget this day happened and let's move forward."

From that day forward Yvette and Jazzy never discussed that day again. By taking her daddy's life, Jazzy learned the meaning of always protecting your family by any means necessary.

* * * * *

"They got him. They want money and they will not return him until the debt is paid off," Jazzy said frantically.

"Wait, what are you talking about? Who got him? Who wants money," Cornbread asked with a confused look on his face.

"I don't know exactly who has him Cornbread. All I know is some bitch called me saying she have my man and they wanted money for his return." She went into details about the phone conversation she had with ol' girl. She didn't leave anything out. She made sure she covered all of the bases, hoping Cornbread might know who had her man.

"This shit doesn't seem right. $200,000? Who in the hell is Ferrari in debt with?"

Jazzy shrugged her shoulders while Cornbread continued to talk. He raised his voice a notch as he spoke because he was pissed that someone had the audacity to kidnap his friend.

"This has to be some thirsty nigga looking for a quick come up. They see him riding around in a Maserati, nigga stay fresh, nice crib and they think a nigga rich. A nigga is doing alright, but a nigga ain't rich. Don't worry, sis, we going to get him back. I got $15,000 stashed away at the crib.

I'm going to go grab that. How much money do you have?"

"I have about $5,000 lying around," Jazzy responded.

"Have you checked Ferrari's stash?"

Jazzy broke eye contact with Cornbread and her eyes wandered to the floor, "Yeah, I checked it. That was the first thing I did when I got off the phone with ol' girl."

"Okay, cool. How much money did he have?"

"Shit, the nigga don't have any money. All the money he had is gone."

"Gone? What the fuck is this nigga doing? What has he gotten himself into?" Cornbread barked.

"I don't have the slightest clue. Whatever it is, we are going to fix it though, "Jazzy stated. Her voice began to crack. "Whatever I have to do to get my man back home, believe me, it will be done."

She was trying her best to hold back the tears, but they fell anyway. One tear fell down each cheek. Cornbread saw the pain in her eyes. He whipped each tear away as they fell down her face, then he kissed her on her forehead and held her tightly.

While Cornbread held Jazzy in his arms, he thought about who could have possibly kidnapped Ferrari. He thought about all their enemies and the list was long. They had so many enemies and haters in the streets that he didn't know where to start. No one stood out. Any one of the niggas he thought of could be behind this.

"Check this out sis…with the cash I got and the cash you got, that's a total of $20,000. That's a start. We need $180,000 more. The block doing alright so we should have the rest of the money in no time."

"Don't forget what I told you she said. She told me that everything don't have to be paid in cash. Don't wreck you brain on that $180,000. I'm going to take her that $20,000 when I meet with her tomorrow. That's one step closer to getting him home. "

"Yeah, I heard what you said, but I don't trust that shit so I'm going to do what I have to do to get that cash. Plus, there's no telling what she might ask you to do. Since my homie not here, I have to keep you out of harm's way."

Cornbread tapped his hand under her chin to raise her head so she could be eye level with him, "I'm staying the night with you in case some more shit pop off."

CHAPTER THREE

Time was 8:45 a.m. when Jazzy's phone rang. She woke up instantly from her light slumber. She rubbed her hand across her bed looking for her phone as it continued to ring. She was a little discombobulated from the lack of sleep and from being mentally drained. All she wanted was her man back home and for things to go back to normal.

Cornbread sat wide-awake across the room in a chair. Through bloodshot eyes, he watched Jazzy as she searched for her phone. He hadn't gotten any sleep at all that night. There was no way he could rest peacefully knowing that his homie was in the hands of the enemy. There have been plenty of nights Cornbread stayed up chasing a dollar so having no sleep didn't bother him one bit.

"Hello," Jazzy said after finding her phone that was buried under her covers. She had a disappointing tone in her voice after she didn't hear ol' girl's voice on the other end of the phone. It was Sharae. She was Jazzy's best friend and also one of Cornbread's chicks. Cornbread had plenty of women in his life and they all knew about each other. Cornbread was a modern-day pimp, except his women weren't fucking other niggas and bringing him the cash; he was fucking them himself and they were giving him whatever they thought he needed. He didn't want for shit though. Females felt like buying him things would help them get closer to his heart, but that never worked. He was a real man; he kept it one hundred with the ladies. It was no secret that he wasn't ready to be in a committed relationship and if they couldn't accept being his fuck buddy, then they could move on. The moment they couldn't handle their position in his life and they wanted more, Cornbread would cut them off instantly.

"Don't give me that ol' dry ass tone. Are we still on for tonight? I went shopping yesterday and bought me a badass dress from Honesty's Closet, my girl Sophia looked out for me. I got a hair appointment at twelve with Swag-Boy, after that, I'm going to pamper myself by getting a facial, my nails done and also my feet. I'm so thirsty to hit the club that I got my outfit laid out on the bed already; it's just waiting for my skin to touch it."

"Sharae, I can't go to Blue Kiva tonight."

When Cornbread heard Sharae's name, he got Jazzy's attention and mouthed the words, "I'm not here." Jazzy cracked a halfhearted smile.

"What you mean you can't hit the club? Girl it's Friday. Let's go get our twerk on," another voice said. It was her other bestie, Tanya. Jazzy didn't realize that Sharae had called her on three-way.

"What's good, Tanya?" Jazzy said with a little bit more spunk. "I haven't seen your ass in about a week."

"You know how it is sometimes. That good dick is keeping me in the house and since you haven't seen me, that's more than enough reason to get your butt out the house tonight."

"Seriously y'all, I have a problem on my hands that needs to be addressed immediately so no playtime for me for about a month. I'm on a straight grind."

"Grind? Girl, cut it out. You got a whole nigga over there that takes good care of you. Your ass doesn't have to lift a finger, so cut it out!" Sharae blurted out.

"And you always screaming you got problems. We all have problems so let's go get fucked up and forget about everything. That's what

34

the white people do. They drown their problems in liquor," Tanya giggled.

"I'm not trying to hear that shit y'all barking right about now," Jazzy said between yawns.

Switching the subject Sharae blurted out, "By the way, have you seen Cornbread ol' big head ass? I haven't talked to that nigga in two days. Ever since I found out he was fucking my sister's friend and I brought it to his attention, he's been ignoring my calls. I know me and him not a couple, but it's boundaries to this shit. I can accept him fucking other bitches, but the people I know are off limits."

"You and the bitches that Cornbread's fuckin' are the last things on my mind. You my girl, Sharae, but you knew what you were getting into when you started messing with Cornbread. Stop focusing on a nigga that's don't give a fuck about you and I'm going to leave it at that."

Jazzy heard Sharae smack her lips. Sharae knew that Jazzy was telling the truth. She would never steer her friend wrong. She always had her friend's best interest at heart. Jazzy knew her friend could do better, she didn't understand why she put up with Cornbread's bullshit. She had asked Sharae on many occasions, "How can you be faithful to man that doesn't even belong to you?"

All Sharae would ever say was, "He does belong to me, he just don't know it yet."

"I don't care about you smacking your lips, but seriously, I have a major problem. My man has been kidnapped and I have to get him back."

"What? Get the fuck out of here!" Tanya and Sharae blurted out at the same time.

Sharae was cut from the same cloth as Jazzy so she knew the dynamics of fuckin' with a street hustler with major clot. Tanya, on the other hand, wasn't really about that life; she was more so a follower and she fucked with the petty hustlers.

Sharae quickly stated, "I'm on my way over there!" She was literally grabbing her coat as she chatted on the phone.

"Is there anything I can do?" Tanya asked.

"Sharae, stay put. I'm good, sis. Just let me clear my mind and if I need either one of y'all, I will call you. Y'all just need to stay on point."

"Cool, don't forget to call me if you need me. I'm down for whatever," Sharae said, meaning every word of it.

"I already know. Just keep your phone nearby at all times," and right after that, Jazzy hung up the phone without saying goodbye.

Jazzy was getting impatient as the time ticked away. She caught a migraine thinking about Ferrari. She needed to know that he was alright. She didn't know if he was being beaten every hour on the hour, if they were feeding him or even if they were allowing him to go to the bathroom. She hated to think that her man was being mistreated. On a typical morning, Jazzy would get up and cook breakfast for herself and her man, but not this day, and it was hurting like hell for her to break their everyday routine.

Cornbread looked at Jazzy; he knew she was stressing. It was written all over her face. It didn't take a rocket scientist to see it. Cornbread had mad respect for Jazzy, though. He loved the way she handle herself. She didn't crack when the pressure was on. Any man would kill to have a bitch like that on their team. She was definitely that Bonnie that every nigga dreamt of. She wasn't your average heel wearing, purse carrying, beauty-shop-going type of chick. She was the sit at the table and cook up work, have her nigga back, shot a pistol type of chick; but she always carried herself like a lady. She definitely didn't listen to the street gossip like most females. Maybe it was because most of the gossip was about her and her man.

She knew her place in Ferrari's life. She was secure in her position and a bitch couldn't break that up even if they tried to. Everybody knew that Ferrari was very much in love with Jazzy because no matter what he asked her to do, it was done with no questions asked. There was never any back talk. She allowed Ferrari to be the man that he was. She knew her place as a woman. He was the King and she was his Queen. As long as he treated her as such, she was all-good. Cornbread also loved the fact that behind her feminine ways, Jazzy was built like a nigga. She showed very little emotion when she was around others and by looking at her, one would have never thought that she would kill a nigga in a heartbeat.

* * * * *

Two hours had passed and there was still no call. Jazzy was still in the bed. She couldn't move. Her body ached all over. The pain from her heart shot through her entire body. She wanted to go back to sleep in hopes that when she woke back up, it would all be a dream; but that never happened. Sleep wasn't an option at this point. Reality had set in more than ever and it wasn't allowing her to ease her mind. She hated playing this waiting game. She wanted to do more, but she couldn't and it was tearing her up inside.

Jazzy looked over at Cornbread as he still sat in the chair. He had finally closed his eyes and dozed off. His long legs rested in the center of her bed. His body was slouched over a little, while his head dangled to the side. Jazzy eased out of bed and stood over him. She tapped him on the shoulder and called his name at the same time.

"Cornbread," she said softly, but loud enough not to startle him. He didn't answer. She knew that he was tired and he needed the rest, but she had shit on her mind and she needed to talk. She called out his name again, but this time she shook him. His eyes opened and then closed. She shook him again, this time he woke up completely.

"What's up, Jazzy," he said while clearing his throat and rubbing his eyes.

"This bitch still hasn't called and it's bothering me. Maybe they said fuck the money and killed him."

"I can't see that happening, sis. They need that bread, that's why they kidnapped him. Believe me, for $200,000 they will be calling sooner than later."

"I hope so. I'm so ready to get this over with and this is only the beginning."

"Please, believe we are going to get him back sooner than you think," Cornbread said meaning every word of it.

Jazzy left him to his next thoughts and tried to take his words for what they were, but she couldn't. No words were going to bring her man back home, only action. She walked to her closet, grabbed her housecoat, and headed to the bathroom. She needed to take a shower to clear the fogginess that was clouding her head. She couldn't think straight for anything in the world. No matter how she tried to shake the thought out of her head that her man had been kidnapped, it just wouldn't disappear.

Twenty minutes later, Jazzy was out of the shower and ten minutes after that her phone began to ring. "It's Ferrari's phone calling," she yelled through the house to get Cornbread's attention. He had gone into Ferrari's man cave to see if he left any signs behind on who had abducted him.

"Toss me the phone. I got this," he said as he entered her bedroom. Jazzy did just that and watched as he put the phone up to his ear.

"Yeah," was all Cornbread said into the phone.

"Cornbread, put Jazzy on the phone," the female voice demanded.

"Bitch, stop saying my name like you know me. You don't know me from a can of paint. What you need to be doing is stating your fucking name," Cornbread said with pure anger. Not only was he upset the chick had Ferrari, but he was upset that it felt like she had the upper hand and he hated that.

"Nigga, I do know you. I'm God. I know everything," she laughed. "And who I am really don't matter. Now, put the bitch on the phone, my business is with her, not with you!"

"Let me speak to Ferrari so I can know he's okay," he said ignoring what was asked of him.

"So you going to ignore what I just said huh. Okay, I'll put Ferrari on the phone, but after I do that, I'm not speaking with nobody except Jazzy. Once again, my business is with her not you."

Cornbread felt like he could break the bitch down if it was that easy for her to put Ferrari on

41

the phone. He was a man and he felt superior to any woman, but at this moment, the chick really had the upper hand because she had his boy. Cornbread had to play tough, but smart.

He heard her talking to Ferrari from a distance. He couldn't make out what she was saying to him. Then all of a sudden, he heard Ferrari screaming. He sounded like a bitch giving birth. Cornbread didn't know what was going on.

Moments later, the chick got back on the phone. "Listen here motherfucker, you don't call no shots! I'm the shot caller around here. I run this show. You just cost your buddy one of his fingers. All you had to do was listen, but naw, you wanted to act like you running shit! The only person in control of this situation is me. Now thanks to you, I will be sending his finger in a pretty little gift box to his bitch. Don't fuck with me! I'm not to be played with. Now put the bitch on the phone."

Cornbread didn't say another word. He didn't want to cause his homie more pain than what he had already caused him so he did what was asked of him this time. He politely handed Jazzy the phone without telling her the damage he just caused.

"Hello," Jazzy said into the phone.

"How you doing this morning, baby girl?" ol' girl asked Jazzy as if she gave two flying fucks. She didn't care how Jazzy's morning was going. All she cared about was getting some cash in her pockets and a couple of tasks completed so that she and her partner didn't have to get their hands dirty.

"I would be doing better if my man was at home with me."

"Once you do what is asked of you, your man will be home in no time, but before we proceed, let me say this, my business is with you and only you, not anyone else. I talk to you and only you. The moment I start talking to different people, that's when things get complicated and we don't want that right?" The question was rhetorical. She didn't wait for a reply. "Our meeting will be held at Mike Ditka's restaurant in Oak Brook. When you come in the restaurant, just let them know that you are there to meet with Vanity."

"So, I finally get a name?" Jazzy cut her off, but Vanity kept right ahead with her instructions.

"You will need to be there at 2:00 p.m. sharp. If you are one minute late for our meeting, I will call my partner and tell him to torture your man until you show up. Every minute counts so don't take my time for granted. I'm a business woman Mrs. Lady so please take heed to everything I'm saying and come alone."

Jazzy got off the phone all wrapped up in her feelings. She was on an emotional roller coaster, but now wasn't the time to show it. She had one responsibility at this point, which was to get Ferrari home and after that, track the bitch down – along with whoever else was behind this – and kill them. There was no way in the world they were going to get away with this without some type of retaliation.

Jazzy ordered Cornbread to go home to get the $15,000 he had, while she got her money together. She wanted to let Vanity know that she was about business as well. Jazzy got dressed and waited patiently for Cornbread to return with the cash.

A couple hours passed before Cornbread returned to Jazzy's crib. She was still in her bedroom lying across the bed with her $5,000 stacked neatly next to her. There was only an hour left before her meeting with Vanity. When Cornbread walked into the room, he threw a brown paper bag on her bed full of hundreds, fifties, and twenties. She grabbed the bag instantly and bounced off the bed. She went straight to the bathroom – which was attached to her room – reached under the sink and grabbed the small scale from underneath it. She headed back to her room and sat the scale on the bed.

Cornbread just stared on. It wasn't that Jazzy didn't trust him because she did; she trusted him with her life. She just wanted to double check his count so Vanity wouldn't try to be on bullshit after she handed her the duffel bag. Weighing money was a technique she learned from Ferrari when he was pressed for time and at this point, there was no time to count the money out by hand so the scale technique came in handy.

Once she got an accurate count of the money, she threw it in a duffel bag, grabbed her purse and put her small gun in it in case anything jumped off. She put her shoes on and headed toward the door dressed in a simple Juicy Couture jogging suit.

"I'll see you when I get back."

"What you mean? I'm coming with you. I don't trust that bitch," Cornbread said.

"I don't trust her either, but I got this. Just stay here until I get back. She gave specific instructions for me to come alone. I'm going to play by the rules until I can throw a curve ball. This is my man's life that's on the line here so fall back for now, her rules, her way. Trust me, before it's all said and done, she will get a taste of our medicine and the bitch is going to regret every fucking with my man."

Cornbread didn't argue with that. He knew Jazzy was about business, but he didn't know what they were up against. Vanity seemed like she was a deranged chick. He wanted to go with Jazzy so bad, he even contemplating following her, but he remembered what pain he had just caused Ferrari so he fell back like Jazzy said. He wanted to help the situation, not bring more problems to the situation. He stayed put like an obedient child and waited patiently for her return.

CHAPTER FOUR

Cornbread felt helpless, he felt crippled that he wasn't able to do more to help his boy. While Jazzy was out handing business, he needed something to do to pass time. It was time he hit the streets to see if the streets were talking. Somebody had to know something. Ain't no bitch named Vanity just fell out of the sky and kidnapped his homie. There was definitely more to this shit here and he was determined to find out.

Cornbread hit a couple of corners before picking up the phone to call his boy, Meech. He asked Meech if he was on the block and he was. Driving up Laramie and making a left turn on Chicago Avenue, Cornbread drove until he hit Lotus. At Lotus he made another left and pulled over right before the corner of Huron. Meech stood on the corner dressed in all-black from head to toe; black hoodie, black jeans and black Timberlands. His hands were in his pockets as he waited for someone to count out money to him. When Meech noticed Cornbread pull up, he put up one finger to let him know he would be with him in a second.

Meech was a natural born hustler and because of that, he kept his eyes and ears to the street at all times. He knew everything that went on in and out of the hood and if he didn't know something right then and there when someone asked, it would only be a matter of time before he found out. Trust and believe the streets always talked.

Cornbread waited patiently as he sat in his car waiting on Meech. He bobbed his head to one of Chicago's finest, Emone Quadeem. The music blasted throughout the Alpine speakers as Cornbread threw up two fingers to the three fellows who acknowledged him. Emone's song kept blasting through the walls of the car. He was in a zone, rapping Emone's lyrics word for word. Right when Cornbread's favorite part of the song came on, Meech was getting in the car, interrupting Cornbread's flow.

"What's up, my nigga," Meech said. As he got comfortable in the car, Cornbread turned down the music.

"A lot," he paused for a minute. "A lot of bullshit, that's what's up. It's about to be a lot of noise in the city. Before I get into all that...what's up with you?"

"Shit, chilling…chilling…Just trying to live to see another day and make sure every day I'm here, I'm richer than the day before."

"I know that's right," Cornbread said, then pulled away from the curb.

"So, what's going on? This shit has to be important. Your ass never comes on the block; not even to pick up your money," Meech approached his next words with caution, "Did I fuck up something? Talk to me, what's good, my nigga?"

"Naw, you good, homie. How's shit going on the block?"

"Shit has been slow. That last batch you and Ferrari gave me wasn't any good. People have been complaining for the last couple of days. We normally make $8,000 a day, now we barely making $500. That's not a good look man, but I'm trying my best to push this bullshit."

"It's all good, Meech. Don't even sell that shit no more. I got some knew stuff coming in tonight, but this drug shit is the least of my concerns right now. I have a bigger problem. Ferrari has been kidnapped.

"What? Kidnapped! Who in the hell did some shit like that," Meech said stunned. Ferrari was his boy as well and he knew that shit was about to get crazy in the city if Ferrari didn't pop back up soon.

"I don't know; that's what I'm trying to figure out. Have you heard anything?"

"Naw, my nigga, I haven't heard nothing. You see I was surprised when you mentioned that a nigga had him. Maybe it's those niggas across Laramie that's behind this. You know they have been hatin' on us for the last couple of weeks because all their customers have been fuckin' with us. Plus, Drew found out I was fucking his bitch Tanya and that's only adding fuel to the fire. Drew's bitch is a cool li'l chick, but she ain't loyal to him at all, which is fine by me because she tells me everything. She tells me his every move so if those niggas got something to do with it, believe me, she will let me know and I'll be the first to pull the trigger.

"Cool…cool, just keep me posted if you hear anything."

Cornbread and Meech hit a couple more blocks. They continued to talk. They talked about what they were going to do to keep the block afloat and they discussed what they were going to do to the motherfucker that was behind Ferrari's kidnapping. They talked that gangsta shit. The average Joe would not have been able to take the conversation about Ferrari's kidnappers.

Finally pulling back up to the block, they sat in the car for about ten more minutes throwing ideas out to one another. Cornbread was the one really doing all the talking and Meech just listened attentively. Next thing they knew, gunshots started to ring out through the air.

Boc...Boc...Boc...

This is the main reason why Cornbread and Ferrari rarely came through the joint because anything was liable to happen.

"What the fuck!" Cornbread shouted and ducked at the same time. He told Meech to open his glove compartment and pass him his banger. Meech didn't hesitate. He gave Cornbread his gun and Meech reach in his waistline and pulled out his.

"Do you see that li'l motherfucker right there?" Meech pointed out to Cornbread.

"Right where?"

"Look between the brown building and the yellow house."

Cornbread's eyes focused in that direction and he saw exactly what Meech was talking about. There was a nigga in the gangway dressed in a white t-shirt, a pair of blue jeans, and a New York baseball cap. The nigga was letting his heater do all the talking. They couldn't believe this nigga, though. He had a lot of fuckin' nerve coming on their territory in broad daylight without even covering his face. That was a bold move. When Meech got a good look at the dude, he knew exactly who it was. It was Drew's jealous, hating ass.

Boc...Boc...Boc...

Three more gunshots went flying in their direction. This time, after those three shots they made their way out of the car. Cornbread eased out the car first, but he moved swiftly, leaving the door open for Meech. He crawled over the seat, getting out on the driver side. They ducked on the side of the car until Drew was finished letting off his rounds. As soon as the shots stopped, they headed in the direction of the gangway.

Boc...Boc...Boc...Boc...Boc...Boc...

The gunshots sounded like they were never going to stop. It sounded like the fourth of July. Between the two of them firing their guns nonstop, Cornbread and Meech let off sixteen rounds, emptying their clips. They both hoped that Drew had caught a couple of slugs, but he hadn't. Drew was fast on his feet. By the time they got all the way up on the gangway, he was gone. God was definitely with him, but Meech was going to make sure that God didn't have his back next time. Next time, Drew would have a permanent date with the devil.

Cornbread and Meech heard police sirens from afar. They didn't panic, they kept their cool. Meech noticed a crowd had formed around a body across the street from where he and Cornbread stood. He rubbed his hand across his face and then shook his head.

"Not another brother gone," Meech figured it was one of his worker's that was shot.

"We got to get the fuck out of here," Cornbread said. "Fuck that nigga, we can't do shit for him right now."

"Give me one minute. Give me your gun," Meech demanded.

Cornbread handed him his gun without hesitation.

"It's about to be hot as fuck around here. You know we can't be riding around with this heat on us. Two black niggas in a car with hoodies on…you know we are liable to get pulled over and going to jail right now isn't an option."

Meech then took off in the direction of the body trying to see who the shot person was and Cornbread took off in the opposite direction toward the car.

"Hurry up, nigga. You got one minute to get back to my car. If you not back in that time frame, I'm leaving your ass on this hot ass block," Cornbread yelled from across the street.

Meech didn't say anything; he just walked toward the body. The closer he got to the body; he began to recognize a cry coming from the crowd. The cry was so familiar to him. He knew that cry from anywhere because he had been the reason for the tears on many occasions. It was his baby momma Caprice.

What the fuck is she doing over here, he thought. They weren't together and she knew better than to be popping up on the block before calling. Before he got up to the body, he called out to a young chick he was fucking that stayed on the block and she came running in his direction. He gave her the guns and told her to put them up. She grabbed the guns, looked at him with tears in her eyes and said, "I'm sorry."

"Why in the hell are you sorry," he asked suspiciously.

She didn't say anything; she just put both guns in her oversized Michael Kors purse and walked in the directions of her house with tears streaming down her face.

As Meech got closer to the body, he saw a pair of small feet with Jordan's on. Through the cracks in the crowd, he saw his baby momma on bended knee. He took off running in that direction and pushed whoever was in his way out of the way.

"Not my baby!" she cried out.

Meech stood there in a daze. It felt like his soul had escaped his body as he stared down at his son's lifeless body. Drew's bad aiming ass had taken Meech son's life at the age of four. This was one death sentence Drew wouldn't be able to escape because Meech had it out bad for him now.

When Cornbread caught rift of what was going on, he got out the car and tried to comfort his homie. No words were going to be able to sooth the pain that his buddy was feeling. Only revenge and that was only a temporary fix. First Ferrari, and now this; this can't be life.

Cornbread knew that Meech needed to be with his baby momma so he left him by her side and told Meech to call him if he needed anything.

Cornbread couldn't stand the police so he had to get from off the block quick.

Cornbread needed a stress reliever and he needed one fast. He was fucked up because he couldn't believe that somebody had the audacity to take his boy and on top of that, some bitch ass nigga was shooting at him and Meech trying to take them out and ended up taking out a shorty. Cornbread wanted to be there when Meech road down on that nigga Drew, but his first priority right now was Ferrari. He was starting to feel pissed at Ferrari as the time ticked away for not coming to him to let him know that he was in debt. He was even more pissed because they were partners and that meant that Ferrari had been doing some extra hustling on the side.

Cornbread felt a little betrayed by his boy because they always made moves together. He felt if Ferrari wanted to branch off on his own, he should have come to him and let him know. Owing a motherfucker $200,000 seemed like somebody fronted Ferrari a lot of drugs and Ferrari fucked something up big time; but how? Cornbread thought to himself. Ferrari is the one who taught him the game. Ferrari knew all the tricks when it came to hustling, but what fucked Cornbread up

56

the most was that he and Ferrari had talked about everything and he couldn't understand why he wouldn't come to him about this.

Cornbread drove with no particular destination in mind. By the time he looked up, he was pulling in front of Sharae's house. He grabbed a park and cracked his window a little to get some fresh air circulating in his car while he smoked a cigarette. He sat in front of her house for a while and thought some more about what the fuck Ferrari could have done that was so bad that it could have lead up to this point. Thinking about that shit really had him upset and he was so ready to take his frustration out on somebody. Just like his boy had come to his rescue when them li'l niggas was at his ass in the rec room, now it was time Cornbread returned the favor. He was going to save his boy's life.

As Cornbread sat in front of Sharae's crib a little longer, he realized that he didn't want to be bothered with her or any other bitch right now. None of them could serve as a stress reliever; they were only going to add fuel to the fire. He fucked with a bunch of drama queens. All they were going to do was nag him and he didn't want to snap out on anybody. He was going to serve as his own stress reliever. He had been in jail plenty of times so he knew how to please himself. He pulled off from in front of Sharae's crib, found a nice secluded block, and jacked his dick off. Right after that, he decided to go back to Jazzy's crib.

CHAPTER FIVE

One the other side of the city, Vanity prepared herself for her meeting with Jazzy. She only stayed ten minutes away from the restaurant. She had a brief conversation with her partner and then she headed toward the door. She was stopped in her tracks as she caught a glimpse of herself in the mirror. She was intrigued with herself. Vanity was a pretty li'l bitch and she knew it. She was a mixed chick. Most mixed chicks have an exotic look about themselves and Vanity wasn't short stopping. She was mixed with Asian and Black. Her Black genes were definitely stronger than her Asian genes. There wasn't any Asian chick walking around with an ass like hers. Her slanted eyes were the only thing that revealed there was Asian blood flowing through her veins. Vanity stood just a tad bit over 5'5" and she weighed about a hundred and fifty-five pounds, with an attitude of a giant and much swag. She gave herself another look then she headed out the door.

It was 1:30 p.m. when she pulled into Mike Ditka's parking lot. She arrived thirty minutes early to make sure there weren't any unexpected guests. She circled the parking lot three times before she found a park not too far from the entrance. She sat in her rental car as she waited for Jazzy to pull up. She paid close attention to every car that came in. She was definitely going to spot Jazzy before Jazzy spotted her on the simple strength she was in a different car. She wouldn't dare be in the same car twice knowing what she was up to. This time, Vanity was in an all-white Camry. She had to make sure not to be caught slipping. She knew that Jazzy would be looking for the black car when she arrived.

At 1:50 p.m. Jazzy pulled in the parking lot. She pulled in the first spot she saw. She got out the car with her duffle bag on her arm and then headed toward the door; Vanity wasn't too far behind her. Jazzy's heels met the pavement in a rhythm-like pace.

Upon entrance into the restaurant, Jazzy walked up to the hostess, "I'm meeting someone here. Her name..."

"Excuse, me," Vanity cut her off, "Table for two please." She then looked at Jazzy, "I was running behind schedule. I see you beat me here. Good job."

Jazzy looked Vanity over, she wanted to break her foot off in Vanity's ass, but she remembered that her man was held captive somewhere so she had to keep her cool. When the time came, she knew that going toe to toe with Vanity wasn't going to be no biggie. They both were just about the same height and weight.

"Right this way," the overweight hostess said.

Vanity smiled, showing off her pearly whites. She followed the hostess and Jazzy followed behind Vanity. The restaurant wasn't that crowded, but the few onlookers that were there glanced as the two ladies walked by on their way to their table.

"Your waiter will be with you shortly," the hostess said, then walked away.

"Nice to finally meet Ferrari's ride-or-die chick, I've heard so many things about you. I guess the things he has said about you are true. You must really love this nigga. Most bitches would have said fuck that nigga and kept it moving; but not you, and I respect you for that," Vanity said as she reached her hand across the table for a handshake.

"I'm not your friend so put your hand away and you can keep the small talk. I'm here for one reason and one reason only and that's to get my man back."

"Damn, li'l mamma, you my type of bitch! Ready to handle business, that's what's up. I wish your man was more business orientated like you are. If he was, he wouldn't be in the situation he's in now. Once all of this is over with, maybe you can come work for me. I need a chick on my team who can carry her own weight. Someone who isn't scared to get their hands dirty if need be and most importantly, someone who knows the true meaning of loyalty."

"I'm not trying to hear that shit you talking, Vanity. I told you to stop with the small talk. I'm here for one thing and one thing only. Now can we get to business?"

"I see you're a li'l feisty li'l something. I like that," Vanity said as she licked her lips.

Just by their brief conversation, Jazzy could tell that Vanity was a carpet muncher. She love pussy, but she would take some dick from time to time. Jazzy wasn't on that though. She wanted to tell her ass off for coming at her sideways, but she knew she had to keep calm if she wanted to see her man again so she took control of the conversation.

"First things first," Jazzy said. "In this duffle bag on the floor, there is $20,000 in it."

Vanity clapped her hands together lightly. "Good girl. You are one step closer to getting your man back."

"Don't 'good girl' me. I'm not a fuckin' pet!" Jazzy said heated.

The waiter came over and interrupted their small talk. "Can I get you ladies anything to drink? And are you ready to place your orders?"

"I won't be eating. I don't have an appetite, just water for me," Jazzy replied.

Blocking everything out that Jazzy just said, the waitress spoke again with a huge grin on her face. "Oh, I didn't even notice this was you sitting here. Good afternoon, my favorite customer," Vanity greeted the girl with a pleasant smile. "I know exactly what you want. Your order will be up soon," then the waitress walked away.

Jazzy sat across the table looking at Vanity as if she was a foreign object. Who is this bitch? She thought to herself. This bitch definitely comes here often in order for the waitress to know who she is. While Jazzy was deep in thought, she made a mental note of the waitress's name tag and stored it in her memory bank because she would be back to holler at her on a later date.

"Let's hurry up and get this over with," Vanity said, breaking Jazzy's train of thought. "I'm going to give you four simple tasks to do. Once you have completed everything that has been asked of you, I need you to call Ferrari's phone so we can move forward. I don't care what order you complete them in. All I care about is that you complete all of them. All things must be done within a month. That's four weeks so you can complete a task a week if you want to. Hell, you can do it all in one day. Like I said before, all that matters is that the job is complete; no ifs ands or buts about it. Also, while it's fresh on my mind and so it won't come as a surprise to you, the cash amount that you have to hand over to me is $80,000 since you already gave me $20,000 today and that's due at the end of the month as well. Do you understand?"

All Jazzy could do was shake her head. A $100,000, she thought. She couldn't believe this bitch had a price tag on her man's head. Vanity slide Jazzy a sheet of paper and an envelope. The sheet of paper was a list with the tasks that Jazzy had to complete and the envelope contained pictures, along with some additional information relating to the victims. Jazzy took a deep breath before her eyes glanced over the list. The first thing on the list seemed doable and so did the second and third. There wasn't anything so far that she couldn't handle; but when her eyes landed on the fourth thing on the list, her heart damn near stopped. She yelled out, "I can't do that! Hell no, I can't do no shit like that!" and she slide the paper back over to Vanity.

"Lower your voice," Vanity said through clinched teeth. All eyes were on them when Jazzy blurted out what she couldn't do; but seconds later, the onlookers were back to enjoying their lunch. "Either you do it or you can kiss your boyfriend goodbye. I don't need to keep going over what will happen to your guy if those things are not complete. If you can't handle the things that are ask of you, you need to have all of my money by the end of the night and if you can't, just let me know now so I can call my partner and have him put Ferrari to sleep. I know you got mad love for your guy and I know you don't want to see anything happen to him because if you didn't care for him, you wouldn't be here. Now, do what is asked of you and show your man just how deep your love is."

Jazzy got up from the table with a frown etched on her face and Vanity's eyes followed with a huge grin on hers. She watched as Jazzy exited the restaurant. Vanity just sat there waiting for Jazzy to return. She knew Jazzy hadn't gone far because her man's life was in her hands. Seconds later, Jazzy returned with a much calmer demeanor. She didn't take a seat. She simply grabbed the list that she had pushed over to Vanity and then she grabbed the envelope that rested on the table. She told Vanity that she would be in touch and she left the restaurant without looking back. She didn't stick around for her water. There wasn't nothing else left to be discussed between the two. The only thing that was left to do was get on top of her business.

As soon as Jazzy was in her car, she pulled out her cell phone and called Sharae.

"I need for you to meet me at my crib. Shit is about to get real."

"I'm on my way," Sharae assured her friend. She liked getting down and dirty so what Jazzy said was music to her ears. She knew all about the streets and the consequences that followed if things are not done properly and if her girl was willing to take a risk, she was ready to do the same. She knew how much Jazzy loved Ferrari and whatever it took to get him home, she was down for the cause.

Sharae was one of those rough chicks. She was raised in the projects, but knew how to act when out in public. Unlike Jazzy, Share came from a loving home, but once her mother and father were killed by one of the local drug dealers for being the project's snitch, she was left for the streets to raise. Right after her parents' death, she did what she had to do to stay afloat. She refused to be a ward of the State so she begged her dope-fiend aunt to take her in. Still living in the projects, Sharae began to get mixed up with the wrong crowd; a crowd that her parents would have never approved of. She sold drugs from time to time and did some occasional fucking and sucking to make ends meet because the checks that her aunt received for her every month went right to the dope man.

Sharae was a girl all alone in this cruel world, but she got lucky and fell in love with a drug dealer who took her out of the projects. He taught her all about the street life and what it took to be a drug dealer's wifey. He went hard for her and she went twice as hard for him until he was found murdered. The same love Sharae had with her man, she sees in Ferrari and Jazzy. That's the main reason why she stands behind her girl.

Jazzy pulled up to her crib about thirty minutes later. When she saw Cornbread's car in her driveway, her stomach balled up in knots. She missed her man and having Cornbread around her wasn't making things any better. Cornbread reminded her so much of Ferrari; from the way he talked, down to the way he acted. She took a deep breath, threw her car in park, and got out. While walking to her front door, she saw Sharae's car pull up and hug the curb. Sharae got out the car dressed ready for war. Her hair was pulled back in a ponytail, she was dressed in a Nike jogging suit, and her feet were complimented with a pair of comfortable Air Max. Hanging across her body was a small Louis Vuitton purse, just the right size for her prize possession, her baby .22.

Once Sharae and Jazzy were in the crib, they saw Cornbread sitting on the living room couch. He had a fifth of Peach Ciroc resting on the table and a shot glass in his hand. With the type of day he had, he needed that drink. His eyes were glossy as hell. Jazzy knew that he was drunk. She felt like cursing his ass out for getting drunk at a time like this, but she didn't because she needed a drink herself as well. Instead of going into the kitchen to grab a glass to drink out of, she snatched the bottle off the living room table and turned that bitch upside down.

Sharae looked at Cornbread with disgust. She didn't say a word to him. She wanted to lash out at his ass, but it wasn't about her and him at this time; it was about Jazzy and Ferrari.

Jazzy felt the hostility between the two of them so she went right ahead with the business at hand.

"Cornbread and Sharae, I'm glad that y'all are here. This bitch, Vanity, is a trip!"

"Who the fuck is Vanity?" Sharae asked amongst her confusion. She didn't have the slightest clue about the meeting Jazzy had just had with Vanity; all she knew was Ferrari had been kidnapped.

Very quickly, Jazzy briefed Sharae on what was going on. Sharae couldn't believe her ears. She knew the streets didn't play fair, but damn…with the amount of money that Ferrari seemed to owe to Vanity, anyone could live a comfortable life. All Sharae said was, "Let me at the bitch first, Jazzy…because I know you are going to kill her once you get your hands on her. I want to let her know that bitches like us don't play games over our men. Once I'm through with her, the word 'kidnap' won't be in her vocabulary."

Jazzy knew that Sharae meant every word she said. That's why they clicked so well. She wasn't for none. They were down for each other as if they were real family. Jazzy and Sharae had been friends for the last twelve years and there wasn't anything in the world that could break the two apart.

Jazzy picked up where her conversation ended. "There are three things that Vanity wants me to complete and they need to be completed within three weeks," Jazzy lied without thinking twice about it. She wouldn't dare share with Cornbread or Sharae the last thing that was on her to-do-list. She had to tackle that task alone. "I need both of y'all to help me with this, and I still have to come up with $80,000."

"Don't worry about the money, I got that covered; but what is this shit she wants you to do?" Cornbread asked very concerned.

"We need to hit the road with the very first task."

"Where we going?" Sharae asked.

"We are going to Wisconsin. This bitch said there is a nigga out there that owes her some bread, and he has been dodging her. All we have to do is go out there, rob his ass and push his wig back. That's basically two jobs in one. Once the job is completed, we are one step closer to getting Ferrari home."

"So when do we leave?" Sharae asked.

"We need to hit the road ASAP. We are leaving Chicago tonight; there is no time to waste. Vanity walked over to the couch and took a seat. She reached in her purse and pulled out the envelope that Vanity had given her at the restaurant.

For the first time, her eyes made contact with the dude's pictures they were going to take out, his home address and the places he normally hung out at. Jazzy basically had his life in her hands.

Jazzy passed his pictures around after she looked at them so they all could get a look at their target. He had a distinctive look about himself, one that stood out through his pictures. He was a brown skin dude, with a big mole on his right cheek; he had a thuggish appearance that screamed I'm a killer so Jazzy made a mental note of that. His chiseled features and long dreads made him just about every woman's dream man. Jazzy hated that she had to kill dude, but she had to do what she had to do to get her man back home.

"This bitch got us doing her dirty work. We are about to have a murder on our hands for a bitch we don't even know. This bitch has lost her mind! If Ferrari wasn't my guy, I would say fuck this shit," Cornbread said.

He was beyond pissed. He was still upset that Ferrari didn't let him know he was in debt. Cornbread decided that he wasn't going to keep pondering on that. He just took it as some people keeping things to themselves because they didn't want their love one involved. It's usually for their safety.

"Cornbread, if you want to keep your hands clean, you don't have to tag along because with you or without you, I'm going to get my man back home."

Sharae looked at Cornbread and didn't hold back. "He got bitches and pussy on his mind," Sharae said sarcastically meaning every word of it.

"Fuck you, bitch. I don't even know why you are here. Do what you do best and come suck this dick." Cornbread grabbed his cock as he spoke disrespectfully to her.

"Alright you two, calm down and cut this bullshit out. This shit is bigger than what you two have going on. I need you both like I said, but Cornbread, if you don't want to get your hands dirty, believe me, there will be no hard feelings," Jazzy spoke sounding a little agitated.

"Sis, I didn't mean it like that, trust me. I'm down for the cause, but make sure you keep that bitch away from me," Cornbread stated as he pointed at Sharae.

"I'm sorry, Jazzy, but I have to get this off my chest," she looked Cornbread dead in his eyes, "You no pussy eating, big dick with no strokes having ass nigga...trust me, I don't want to be near your sorry ass. I will make sure I keep my distance because being around you makes my pussy dry."

"Enough! And I'm not going to say it anymore. Y'all have no other choice, but to be around each other if we are going to get this shit done. Think about Ferrari y'all. He needs us and I need y'all."

Sharae felt bad for her actions. She walked over to her girl and gave her a hug. "Anything for you," she said.

When Jazzy hugged her girl, she felt the sincerity behind the hug. She knew her girl had her back no matter what; but she also knew that her girl was hurting deep down inside because she wanted more than what Cornbread was willing to give.

Jazzy looked at her watch, it was now 5:30 p.m. "Well, y'all...I want to be on the road by 10:00 p.m. I'm about to go pack my shit and I suggest y'all do the same. Meet me back here at 9:30 p.m.

Cornbread simply nodded his head and Sharae said, "Okay." They both left out the door headed in separated directions, but with the same agenda.

Jazzy sat on her couch a little longer before she busted a move. Her head rested against the back of her couch as her eyes focused on the ceiling. Her eyes fixated on the ceiling fan above that blew out cool air. She was stuck in a daze. She missed her man. She felt alone at this point. Even though she had Sharae and Cornbread, she knew it wasn't nothing like her man's love. Breaking out of her daze, Jazzy's eyes rotated around the room as it zoomed in on the pale paint. She giggled to herself a little as she reminisced about an argument she and Ferrari had about paint. She wanted to paint the room purple, but he wanted pale so they had a bet that whoever could make the other cum the fastest, got to paint the room the color they wanted it. Of course Ferrari won, making Jazzy cum in less than five minutes with his tongue. They had so many memories together; inside that house and outside of it. She knew if the shoes were on the other foot, Ferrari would kill the world if he had to so she wouldn't dare let him down. Jazzy knew that he loved her just as much as she loved him.

* * * * *

Cornbread gave Meech a call, "Yo, Meech...how you feelin' my nigga?"

"I'm fucked up, homie. My li'l man is gone. You know I immediately got on Drew's heels. I went through his block and shot that bitch up. I didn't see him out there though, but I had to send a message. I hit two niggas that was sitting in the park. Every time I see a nigga at the park, I'm

75

going to let they ass have it. Drew's bitch, Tanya, told me that he skipped town so I just have to be patient and wait until he returns."

"If you need some more manpower just let me know, 'cause you know I fucks with you. I know you just lost your son and all, but like I told you earlier, I have a new batch coming in and I'm about to hit the road tonight. If I don't have that shit in my hands by the time I leave, I'm going to need you to bust a move for me real quick. What my connect normally does is, he leaves my package in an undisclosed location and once my order is ready, he calls me with the location. All I'm going to need for you to do is go pick it up, cook it up and put it out on the streets. Do you think you can handle that?"

"The shit you asking me to do I can do with my eyes closed," Meech stated, sounding pumped up even though he was heartbroken.

"I'm trusting you, my nigga. The money doesn't stop because I'm going out of town. I have to come up with $80,000 to get Ferrari back so make sure you push that shit to the limit," with a stern voice Cornbread barked, "Don't fuck up, I'm counting on you!" then he soften his voice a little, "and you know I'm going to look out for you big time on this. I'm only going to be gone for a couple of days. I will be checking in on you periodically to make sure things are running smoothly. And has ol' girl given you any indications that the niggas across Laramie had something to do with Ferrari?"

"I'm almost certain them niggas didn't have anything to do with it. They get a pass on that… but they are going to feel the heat for my son."

"Wait, you said ol' girl's name is Tanya; right?"

"Yeah, why? What's up?"

"Are you talking about Tanya with the big bootie and big titties? The one be pushing that Lexus?"

"Yeah, I'm talking about her."

"This shit crazy…it's a small world. Tanya is best friends with Ferrari's girl. She doesn't come around too often so I never knew who she fucked with. She needs her ass beat for fuckin' with that lame ass nigga, Drew, but anyway, keep your phone by you at all times. If I need you to handle that business or not, you will be getting a call from me either way."

"Cool," Meech replied.

"Now let me go do what I have to do. I'll holla at you in a few, my nigga. One love!" Then Cornbread hung up the phone.

CHAPTER SIX

Milwaukee, Wisconsin was only an hour and a half from Chicago. It was 10:45 a.m. when they arrived. They decided that since Wisconsin was so close to home, there was no need to leave the night before; so when Sharae and Cornbread returned, they camped out at Jazzy's crib. They all woke up feeling refreshed and ready to handle business. The road trip went smooth, even though they were riding dirty. Each carried a gun and if they got pulled over they all were going to jail; especially Cornbread because he had a warrant out for his arrest. There was minimal talk on their way there, except when Cornbread was giving orders to Meech over the phone because his connect didn't come through that night like he was supposed to. That morning, his connect called him informing him where the package would be.

After Cornbread got off the phone with Meech, they all thought about the crime they were going to commit; but they didn't regret what they were about to do because it was for a good cause. Cornbread's hair rose on the back of his neck each time he thought about pulling the trigger, but what bothered him the most was Vanity's character. He wanted to get up close and personal with her. He wanted to see if she was just as tough, face-to-face, as she was over the phone. Cornbread was raised not to hit a woman, but this was one chick that he was going to knock the fuck out.

Sharae really didn't put much thought into what she was about to do. All she knew was that it had to be done. She didn't care about taking another's person life. She felt like her life was over the moment her mother and father died, and the moment when life was brought back to her, it was taken again when her boyfriend was killed. Sharae loved Jazzy more than she would ever know. She was the only family Sharae had, and all Sharae wanted at this point, was to see her friend happy again. Seeing sadness on Jazzy's face made her heart ache. Sharae didn't want Jazzy to experience the heartache she had felt, so she was going to make it her personal mission to make sure every task got completed.

As Cornbread pulled the car into the parking lot of the hotel, he drove right up to the front door, put the car in park, and then popped the truck. Sharae was the first to emerge from the vehicle.

Cornbread looked at her through the review mirror as she exited the car. He knew that she hated him for fuckin' her sister's friend, but he wasn't going to let it bother him because she knew what type of relationship he and she had from the start.

He looked at Jazzy and said, "Everything will be alright."

She replied, "I hope so," with a trace of uneasiness in her voice. Jazzy then got out the car and looked up at the clear blue sky and mouthed the words, "I wish this was all a dream," then brushed her hand across her face. She felt like she was living a nightmare. She felt like her world was falling apart. Two days had passed since she had an actual conversation with Ferrari, and it was killing her so softly.

Walking straight to the trunk of the car, Jazzy grabbed her luggage and Cornbread's suitcase. Jazzy and Sharae walked into the hotel, while Cornbread parked the car. They decided to stay at the Holiday Inn, which was about twenty minutes away from where their target rested his head every night.

"Give me two rooms," Sharae stated to the front desk clerk.

Jazzy added her two cents. "Actually give us three rooms. No offense to you, Sharae, but I need my space. I hope you understand."

Sharae didn't complain at all. She understood. She knew that Jazzy needed some much needed time to herself. Cornbread made his way through the lobby and headed to the desk with Sharae and Jazzy. As soon as he walked up, the front desk clerk handed Sharae all three room keys. She passed both of them a key and they all walked toward the elevator.

"I need to close my eyes for a couple of hours and then freshen up a little; so around 1:30 p.m. I want both of you to come to my room so we can discuss how we are going to handle this."

Cornbread and Sharae both shook their head to let Jazzy know they understood. They got on the elevator and headed to the third floor; once the doors opened, they went their separate ways.

Forty-five minutes had passed before Jazzy heard a knock on her door. Cornbread had crept over to her room. He knew she didn't want to be bothered, but he had to talk to her. He needed to get something off his chest and it couldn't wait any longer. He knocked softly on her door, not wanting Sharae to hear his knocks from across the hall. He knocked several times, but his knocks were not answered. He took out his cell phone and called Jazzy's phone, but it went straight to voicemail. He knew she was stressing about her nigga, but she had never isolated herself from him. He knocked on her door again, but this time louder with each knock. Jazzy swung opened the door without saying, "Who is it." she knew it had to be one of two people because nobody else knew she was there.

"Can I come in?"

Jazzy didn't say a word; she just stepped to the side. He walked into her room that was occupied by a king size bed. All the rooms were identical. Jazzy closed the door behind Cornbread and when she turned back around, she was face to face with him.

"What's up Cornbread?" she said dryly.

"You," he answered. She could smell the liquor on his breath as he spoke loudly.

Jazzy was caught off guard. His focus should have been on Ferrari, not her. He should have been coming in there with some type of game plan to take the nigga out that they were in Wisconsin for.

"What you mean me," Jazzy questioned. She tried to push pass Cornbread, but he wasn't having it. He had her boxed in. He felt like this was going to be his only chance to get what he had to say off his chest. He wasn't going to let her move until he said what he came to say.

The volume in his voice didn't change. "Don't start with all this brand new shit, Jazzy. Ever since Ferrari has been gone, you have been neglecting me. You've been depriving me from my pussy. It's like you taking the shit out on me."

Cornbread's hand reached for her hand. She snatched it away and used all the strength she had and forced her way past him and stood in the area with the bed in it; Cornbread wasn't too far behind her. Pissed by his words, she couldn't believe him or the tone in his voice. She didn't want their conversation to get any louder than what it had already gotten. Hotel walls are known to be thin, and she didn't want Sharae to hear their conversation.

Speaking in almost a whisper, Jazzy said, "Cornbread, I can't do this with you right now. Actually, I can't do this anymore. We were bogus from the start. That's my man and he's your boy."

Cornbread grabbed Jazzy by the arm and pulled her close to him. "Let me tell you something, Jazzy. It will never be over between us. You know how I feel about you. I'm willing to stop fucking all these bitches for you. We haven't been fucking for a year for nothing. That pussy is mine, girl…so stop playing!"

Jazzy broke away from his grip. "Listen to yourself, Cornbread…you sound obsessed and stupid at the same damn time. What we had was nothing but some fucks; nothing more or nothing less…just fucks! We can't be together; not now, not ever. You can have any woman in the world, but your mind is telling your heart to lock in on your guy's girl and that's fucked up."

Cornbread was pissed off. Things weren't going according to plan. He planned on going into Jazzy's room to fuck her brains out so she could get her mind off Ferrari; but Jazzy wasn't having it.

"Maybe Ferrari should stay missing and then I can have you all to myself," he laughed and stumbled at the same time.

"You're drunk and you sound absurd. What makes you think that if I don't get Ferrari back alive, that there will be a me and you? Wait,"

Jazzy got all in his face, "where is my man, Cornbread? Did you have something to do with his disappearance?"

Laughing as if she had just told him the funniest joke in the world, Cornbread grabbed her by the cheeks forcing her to stare deep into his eyes. His glassy eyes weren't the normal eyes she had stared into before. His eyes told a story of betrayal. Jazzy wasn't sure if the betrayal in his eyes were from sleeping with her, or from kidnapping Ferrari.

"Let me tell you something. No pussy in this world will make me kill, kidnap, or bring any harm to my homie. The only thing I'm guilty of is fucking his bitch," Cornbread said.

Cornbread's hands eased from her face. He really didn't want to argue with Jazzy. All he wanted was to feel her hot box. Nothing else matter to him at that very moment.

"For some reason, I don't believe you. You're lying and you know it!" Jazzy quickly reached behind her back and pulled her gun that was resting in her waistline and aimed it at Cornbread's head. "Where the fuck is my nigga and who is this bitch, Vanity? You better get to talking before I let off a round or two in your ass."

Cornbread threw his hands up in the air like the police had just told him to freeze; he then placed his hand gently on the top of his head and dropped to his knees one by one. He moved his head closer to the gun so it would touch it.

"If you really think I had something to do with Ferrari being kidnapped then pull the trigger now!" he yelled, not caring who heard him. Jazzy didn't say a word; she just stared at him with untrustworthy eyes. "Pull the trigger damn it!" he shouted.

Jazzy's heart was beating faster than normal. She was stuck between a rock, and a hard place. She was confused; really confused. She had always trusted Cornbread, but she wasn't sure if she could trust him at this point. Her mind was starting to play tricks on her. Deep down in her heart, she really didn't believe that Cornbread would do a thing like that to Ferrari; but his statement made her second guess his loyalty.

Cornbread saw the doubt in her eyes. He knew that Jazzy knew what type of nigga he was, so he did what any man would do in his situation. He reached up and grabbed the gun from her hands, praying she didn't shoot. He got off his knees, pulled her close to him, and kissed her passionately. Jazzy kissed him back with tears rolling down her eyes. For that brief moment, she felt weak…but she immediately got back focused. Truth of the matter was, Jazzy was in love with Ferrari, but she enjoyed Cornbread's strokes.

"Cornbread, can you please leave? I need to stay focused on one thing at a time, and right now that's Ferrari."

Cornbread didn't argue with her. He merely mouthed the words, "I love you," placed the gun on her bed and left her to herself.

Once Cornbread left the room, Jazzy went straight for the large brown envelope. She sat on her bed, Indian style. She emptied the envelope's contents on the bed and studied dude's pictures as she thought of a plan to execute. The rest that she had planned on getting wasn't going too happened. Cornbread fucked that all up when he came banging on her door. Just as she was coming up with a plan, her cell phone rang; it was Ferrari's phone calling.

"Hello," Jazzy said calmly even though she was agitated.

"What's your room number?"

"Huh?"

"You heard me. What's your room number? I know you are staying at the Holiday Inn. All I need is your room number so I can have this gift delivered to you," Vanity said, with a smile plastered on her face that Jazzy could see through the phone.

"How did you know where I was staying?"

Vanity ignored the question. "What's your room number?"

Not sure what Vanity had up her sleeve, Jazzy reluctantly gave her the room number. "I'm in room 309."

Moments later, there was a knock on her room door while she was still on the phone with Vanity. Jazzy listened to Vanity as she rumbled on about the dude that was to be the first target, whose name Jazzy finally learned was Mel. She thought by Vanity asking her for her room number, that it was her at the door, but she quickly shook that out of her head after the things she heard in Vanity's background. Then she had the feeling that it was Cornbread at the door again. She knew the only way he would act right and give her some space, was if she gave him some pussy. She hated that she had put herself in the situation of fucking friends, but when you have a nigga in the streets making moves, and he's not dicking his chick down like he is supposed to, and his buddy is always coming to the house dropping off money – looking sexy as ever, something is bound to happen between the two.

Jazzy told Vanity that she would hit her back in a second because someone was at her door. Vanity didn't reply. All that was left in Jazzy's ear was dead air. Jazzy hopped off the bed, headed to the door, and looked through the peephole. Her eyes grew big. She thought her eyes were deceiving her so she quickly opened the door. Standing right in front of her, with a gift box in her hand, was the chick, Kenya from Mike Ditka's restaurant . Jazzy had made plans to get up with ol' girl to try to get some information on Vanity, but from the looks of it, that would never happen; at least not the way she planned.

Not saying anything, Kenya walked in Jazzy's room. Kenya was one of the ugliest girls that Jazzy had ever laid eyes on, and from her vibe, Jazzy could tell Kenya had an ugly soul to match. Kenya was a dark-skinned chick that rocked blue contacts and she wore a long weave down the center of her back. The only thing that Kenya had going for herself was a banging body. The bitch's body was Trina bad. She was small up top and well-proportioned on the bottom. Jazzy stared at her strangely because it was like the girl in front of her was a brand new person. Her swag was very different from the cheap uniform threads that touched her body the other day. Kenya was now dressed in a custom-made royal blue and cream jumpsuit with a pair of Salvatore Ferragamo's on her feet. She looked like she was dressed for the club or was about to hit somebody's runway.

Jazzy wanted to ask Kenya a million questions, but decided against it. She knew that whatever question she threw her way, a lie was going to bounce back. The truth of the matter was that the only reason Kenya was working at the restaurant four days a week was to keep her parole officer off her ass. She had just come home from the federal penitentiary for playing checks.

Kenya had made her way in the small kitchenette area and fixed herself a glass of water. The gift box that she had in her hand now rested on the counter top. The silence was killing Jazzy, so she asked a question anyway. She was sure she wasn't going to get an answer at all, but she took a chance.

"How y'all know I was here?"

"A little something called a tracking device gave you away," Kenya quickly replied.

Jazzy was surprised that Kenya answered her question. Kenya told her that while her and Vanity were being seated at their table, she was outside planting the tracking device under her car. When Kenya came to the table to take their orders that was just to let Vanity know that the job was completed.

Jazzy was at a loss for words for the first time in her life. These bitches were on a level that she wasn't ready for. She had to really put on her thinking cap and outsmart these bitches. Since Kenya showed up at the hotel, she figured she was Vanity's partner.

Kenya saw Jazzy eying the gift box. "Oh, yeah…this is for you," she said as she picked the box up and handed it to Jazzy.

Jazzy didn't have a good feeling about the box. She didn't have a good feeling about the whole situation anymore. She wanted to be a ride or die chick for her nigga, but she was starting to think that maybe she was in over her head. Then she heard her mother's voice saying, "protect your family by any means necessary."

Jazzy opened the gift box slowly and Kenya stared on. What she was about to see she wasn't ready for. "What the fuck is this?!" she shouted as she dropped the box. When the box hit the floor, a pinky finger with a diamond ring on it rolled out.

In a devious voice, Kenya said her peace, "You know exactly what that is. I'm sure the diamond ring made it more clear whose finger it was. Don't complete this task and your guy's heart will be mailed to you next."

"I thought y'all said y'all weren't going to hurt him?" Jazzy said in a wining voice.

"You have Cornbread to thank for the finger." Kenya smiled and walked out the door.

CHAPTER SEVEN

When Kenya left the room, Jazzy was rattled up because those bitches was playing dirty, but wanted her to play fair. They cut Ferrari's pinky finger off and it had her feeling powerless. These bitches were on some mob shit. How in the hell did he get mixed up with these two bitches, she wondered, and then she quickly called Sharae and Cornbread and told them to come to her room. Once they were there, Jazzy went over the incident that had just taken place in her room. She didn't even bother to mention to Cornbread that Kenya said he was the blame for the finger. Actually, that was the least of her concerns. There was no time to place blame. All she wanted was her man back home. It was time that she do what she came there to do, but first she had to come up with a plan.

They sat and brainstormed on how they were going to set dude up to kill him, but everything they came up with seemed so far-fetched. Pussy was the number one bait; but the type of nigga Mel was, pussy wasn't going to get it. They threw ideas at each other for about an hour before Jazzy's phone rang again. When she looked at the caller ID it was Ferrari's number calling her again. She was sick of tired of seeing his number pop up on her caller ID when it wasn't the man that she loved on the other end of the phone.

Breathing heavily into the phone, Jazzy greeted Vanity with a simple, "What's up?"

"Kenya told me how you reacted to the finger and I do apologize if we startled you, but I had to let you know that I mean business; but the purpose of this call isn't to talk about the finger. When we first discussed business, I told you that as long as you followed my lead, this thing would run smoothly for you. I know you and your crew probably over there banging y'all heads up against the wall trying to come up with a plan on how to take out dude and by me being a woman of my word, I'm going to do just that…make this very easy for you. I'm going to tell you this one time and one time only, so pay close attention. Mel meets his son at the same time every single day at the barbershop on Forest Home Avenue. His son is a runner for him. You will see his son with a book bag on his back. In that book bag there will be money…lots of money. His son will then hand him the book bag. In exchange for the book bag, Mel will hand his son a duffle bag, which would be full of kilos. Right in the middle of the exchange, you will ambush them. I know I only told you to kill Mel, but fuck it, kill his son too. We don't want to leave any witnesses behind. As soon as you kill them, Kenya will be parked right on the corner in a blue Camaro. Hand her both bags immediately and after that you know what's next."

"Yeah, I know what's next, on to the next task," Jazzy sounded disturbed. "We aren't going to execute the plan today. I want to check out the scene before I do anything. You know…get a feel for things. If he meets his son every day at the same time… tomorrow or the day after tomorrow, it wouldn't make any difference when I handle it. I will call Ferrari's phone when I'm ready."

"I don't care when you do it as long as you get everything done within the timeframe I gave you. From your reaction at the restaurant the other day," Vanity giggled, "you might want to hurry up and get the first three things out of the way because it seems like the last thing on your list is going to be a challenge for you. The quicker you get Mel and his son out the way and then Toby, the guy here in Chicago…the more time you will have to concentrate on your last task," Vanity said.

"I understand all that, but like I said I will call you when I'm ready," Jazzy said sternly.

Jazzy was nervous about everything, but she couldn't show it. She knew she couldn't let Vanity see her sweat even though she had the upper hand. She got off the phone with Vanity and let the others know what they were up against.

Everybody was game. They were just ready to get this over with and head back to Chicago so they could be in their comfort zone. They knew nothing about Wisconsin and didn't trust the people that had them there doing their dirt. They were all hoping that this wasn't a setup to have them killed.

Jazzy looked at her diamond watch that Ferrari bought her as a "just because" gift. It was almost time for Mel and his son to meet up. They all got dressed in their war gear as they called it and headed to their destination. Dressed in all-black hoodies, they sat in their car on the opposite side of the street from the barbershop. The barbershop sat in the middle of the block, so they parked on the corner to get a good view. The barbershop was in the heart of the ghetto. How in the hell were they going to pull this off? Niggas were everywhere. It wasn't too hot or too cold.

The weather was just perfect, so niggas were scattered around like roaches. Whatever they did, they would have to do it quick. They had to time themselves. The faster they moved, the quicker the job would be over with.

Jazzy looked at her watch again, "Mel should be pulling up in a second." Cornbread opened the door to get out the car. "Where are you going," Jazzy asked.

"I'm going to get closer. We need a man on the street as well. Us sitting in this car isn't going to get it. Sitting in this car is painting a different picture than we can get from an up-close point of view. Look at me," he pointed to himself. "I fit right in with those hood-rat looking ass niggas."

Cornbread had a point and he actually did fit it. Each nigga had on a black hoodie; typical clothing for a street hustler. They all looked like nickel and dime hustlers. It was easy to tell that this was a high-traffic drug area. In every direction, hypes were walking up and down the street looking for their next fix. Being from Chicago, Cornbread had a third eye. He was always alert and didn't trust too many, so he had to keep a close eye on them niggas that stood on the corner. If they were anything like him, they were strapped. When he was a corner hustler, he kept his banger on him at all times. He wasn't blind to that fact, and never underestimated a corner hustler. They were always the first to pull the trigger. Those niggas didn't put any fear in him though. He didn't have a scared bone in his body. He knew all about the streets and he was a real street nigga. He lived and breathed this shit every day, but he knew that bullets had no name on them, so he had to play it smart.

As the niggas stood on the corner talking shit and smoking a blunt, they never saw Cornbread get out the car and post up in the alley. Jazzy and Sharae watched as Cornbread eased his way up the streets and posted in the alley that was directly across the street
from the barbershop. The alley cut the block in half. Cornbread stood in the alley with his dick in his hand like he was talking a piss. Staring out the corner of his eyes, moments later he saw a silver drop top pull up. He remembered the picture from Jazzy's envelope and knew that the man driving was Mel. Just like Vanity said, as soon as he pulled up his son appeared out of the barbershop with the book bag in exchange for a

duffle bag. Right after that, his son disappeared behind the doors of the barbershop.

Shaking his dick like he just finished urinating, Cornbread jogged back to the car. He got in and told Jazzy to pull off.

"This shit should be pretty easy…what you think Cornbread?" Jazzy had excitement behind her voice.

"Yes, this is going to be easy, but we still have to play this one smart. Tomorrow we are going to do the same routine, except Sharae, I need you as a diversion. I want you to distract those niggas on the corner because if they are anything like us niggas in Chicago, they strapped and if any gunshots ring out they are going to be busting at our ass. The moment they start busting at me and Jazzy, you need to be busting at they ass. Don't hold back. Let they ass have it. Also, wear something tight and sexy to show off your fat ass. As a matter of fact, wear a pair of leggings. Every nigga love to see a thick chick in a pair of leggings, especially if all the curves are in the right place." Cornbread spoke answering Jazzy question and giving instruction to Sharae at the same time.

"Cool," Sharae said. Even though she was still pissed at Cornbread, she had to put her feelings to the side because as soon as this was over with, she was going to be all over his ass.

In route to the hotel, they stopped off at a drive-thru to grab a bite to eat. Jazzy would have preferred to sit down in a nice restaurant, but they all looked like they were about to set it off. Once back at the hotel, they all piled up in Jazzy's room. Cornbread took out his phone and gave Meech a call because he needed him in Wisconsin ASAP. Once he learned that Kenya was coming to grab the bags, Cornbread would have Meech follow her back to Chicago in hopes that she would go to the location where Ferrari was being held against his will.

"You good, my nigga?" Cornbread asked Meech once he picked up the phone. "What the block looking like?"

"The new batch I picked up is one point. We back on the money," Meech said thrilled.

"Good because I need to get this money together to get Ferrari back…like yesterday."

"Damn, I can't believe them motherfuckers put a price tag like that one his head, but don't worry…I got this shit covered out here. The way the block looking, you will have that in no time." Meche said giving Cornbread hope.

"That's what up, Meech. Keep pushing that shit. I see I taught you well. You mixed up a bomb," Cornbread chuckled. "But my dude, I'm going to need you on something else. I need you to come out her to Milwaukee. I'm out here playing somebody's flunky trying to get Ferrari back home. These motherfuckers got us jumping through loops. They want money and they got us out here committing a 187!" Cornbread went into detail with Meech about the reason he was out there without leaving a single detail out.

"That's some bullshit, man," Meech said pissed.

"Yeah, I know, but you know we out here doing what we have to do to get him home. All you need to do is make sure the block is locked before you leave. Make sure you are here no later than 3:00 p.m. tomorrow, because the move is going down at 4:30. Me, Jazzy, and Sharae are going to do all the dirty work. The only thing you have to do is trail that bitch Kenya back to the city. Make sure you stay on her man. Don't loose her under any circumstance. She's going to be riding back dirty, so make sure the police don't get behind her. I don't want anything to comprise this plan. I'm sure with having the dope and the money, she is going right to where Ferrari is being held. All I need is an address from you and you're free to go back and clock that money. You feel me," Cornbread said briefly.

"Simple shit. I can handle that, boss man," Meech said ready to handle business.

"Cool, my nigga...good looking."

When Cornbread got off the phone with Meech, Jazzy just looked at him and smiled. She liked the fact that he had Meech coming out there because they might be getting her man back sooner than she thought. If those bitches wanted to play dirty, it was time they got down and dirty with them. The three of them chatted and laughed, despite their current situation. They chatted about Ferrari. They all shared their fondest memories of Ferrari like he was a dead man. After a while, Jazzy got tired of all the talk and told her crew that she would get up with them later. Once again they parted ways, leaving each one of them with their own thoughts.

CHAPTER EIGHT

The sun had already risen. It beamed through Jazzy's window and awakened her. She heard the birds chirping and that was her sign that it was going to be a good day. Indeed, spring was in full effect. Before Jazzy got out of her bed, she went to the weather app on her phone to see what the weather was going to be like. Today was going to feel more like a summer day than a spring day, so the war gear was out of the question. The weather was 80 degrees. Niggas tend to act out the hotter the weather is and Jazzy, Cornbread, and Sharae were going to show their ass today. Death was in the air and they could taste it. They were about to catch two bodies and them boys wouldn't even see it coming.

Jazzy got out of the bed and headed for the shower. She stopped in her tracks, turned back around and headed back to her cell phone. She wanted to make the phone call to Vanity to let her know to have Kenya on point. It was going down today, and Jazzy was so ready to get this over with. Once she confirmed everything with Vanity, it was time that she started her day. As she headed back toward the shower, she began to feel butterflies in her stomach. This was the first time in her life that Jazzy had butterflies in her stomach when it came to taking a nigga out. Maybe the butterflies didn't come from that. Maybe it was because Vanity was playing her like a puppet. Vanity held the strings and she was in total control. Jazzy was taking orders and dancing to another motherfucker's beat and she hated every bit of it.

Jazzy's vibe didn't change once she was out the shower. It felt like a black cloud was over her head. When she heard the birds singing as she lay in her bed, she had a feeling that it was going to be a good day; but now her gut was telling her something different. Her gut had never steered her wrong. She dropped to her knees and prayed. She wasn't afraid to talk to the man upstairs, but was it right for her to ask God to watch over her and her team even though they were about to commit the ultimate sin? She knew her God was an understanding and forgiving God, so she went on ahead with her prayer.

After her prayer, Jazzy decided to lie back down for a while. She was mentally drained. She couldn't keep her mind off of Ferrari. She missed him dearly. She missed everything about him. She missed his smooth hands that would rub over her body from head to toe and his soft lips that would touch hers while sending a tingling sensation down to her love box. She wished she had the $200,000 to pay –flat out – to get her man back home; but she didn't, so she had to make certain sacrifices to get back in the comfort of Ferrari's arms.

In the mist of her thinking about Ferrari, Jazzy dozed off, only to be awakened by moaning sounds. For a minute, she thought she dreamt the noise because when she opened her eyes the moans stopped. Trying to get back comfortable, she closed her eyes again and tried to doze back off, but it didn't work. The moans started again and they got louder and louder by the second. She threw the two pillows over her head that were on her bed, trying to drown out the noise, but that didn't help at all. The walls were entirely too thin. The noise was coming through the right wall, which was connected to Cornbread's room. The nerve of this nigga she thought. He was just begging for her pussy and confessing his love to her, and now he was in the next room blowing her friend's back out, but how could she get mad? He wasn't her man. His dick belonged to the community. Sharae moaned with every stroke.

Jazzy found herself getting jealous because she knew the dick was good, but she knew she didn't have the right to be jealous of anything.

Since Sharae was next door getting her pussy popped, Jazzy reached for her purse, opened it and pulled out her small vibrator that was shaped like a tube of lipstick. She kept her ears glued to the wall as she placed the tube of lipstick on her clit. When she turned it on, that motherfucker buzzed like a bumblebee. She placed it on her clit and it sent electrifying chills through her body instantly. She and Sharae moaned in unison, but from different things, yet they were feeling the same pleasure.

"That's enough of this dick, now get on your knees and swallow me whole," Cornbread said loudly. He did it intentionally. Everything he did was intentional. He knew Jazzy could hear through the walls. He wanted her to know that could have been her receiving that good dick.

* * * * *

Back in Chicago, Vanity sat and waited for Kenya to call. She was excited about the money and kilos of drugs they were about to come into. Even though Vanity was born with a silver spoon in her mouth, she loved the hustle. She didn't have to be out in the streets, but she loved the excitement behind it. Vanity's father was a major drug lord in the Philippines, so the hustle was in her blood.

Ripping off Mel was something that Vanity wanted to do for a long time. Truth of the matter was that Mel didn't owe her any money. Vanity used to date him several years back. Actually, they were engaged to be married. Two days before their wedding, he did the unthinkable. That night, which was supposed to be an enjoyable night, had turned into a nightmare for Vanity. Mel had gotten so drunk he handcuffed her to the bed. She didn't think nothing of it because they always had kinky sex, but when he got on his phone and moments later there was a knock at the door, her life would change forever. A crew of men walked into their house, all of which she knew. She didn't understand what was going on at first until Mel told her, "This is my fantasy before I get married. I want to see all five of these men fuck the shit of you." She knew he wasn't thinking right. That shit sounded sick. What man wants to see another man screw his fiancé? He had seemed different lately, but she blew that off as him being stressed about their wedding. The wedding jitter is what she called it. Then all of a sudden, she saw him snort a line. It was all coming together. He was a functioning addict and she was too blinded by love to see it. Mel sat in the cut and watched each man ram his dick in every hole that she had. She felt violated. She felt dirty as she laid there and took each dick without her consent. Vanity never told anybody about this, not even her father. She was too ashamed, but she vowed to get revenge one day and now was the time that she got her victory. Feeling complete again was all that Vanity wanted, and having Mel killed was her road to recovery. In the end, the only thing that mattered after Mel's death was Vanity's closure, and the fact that Jazzy would be one-step closer to getting Ferrari home.

* * * * *

It was show time. Everybody was in their position. Cornbread was in the alley with his dick in his hand, but this time he was on the same side of the street as the barbershop. Cornbread's job was to take out the son. Sharae was walking up the street with her leggings on, showing off her fat ass and thick thighs. She had a messenger bag wrapped around her with her gun in it ready to rock somebody's world, and Jazzy was parked a half a block away waiting for Mel to pull up. Her job was to drive the car, block Mel in, and then take his last breath away from him with one single shot to the head. And just like Vanity said, there was Kenya posted on the corner in her blue Camaro with the engine running. Unbeknownst to Kenya, just a couple of cars behind her, was Meech; parked with his eyes glued to her every move. All of this had to be done in a matter of minutes because they didn't want the police to arrive and fuck up everything. The way they had things planned out though, nothing could go wrong.

As on cue, the silver drop top pulled up. This sun was shining a bit too hard for Mel, so he didn't have the top dropped this day. He was all smiles though, without a worry in the world. If he knew that today was going to be his last day breathing, he would not have had that big Kool Aid smile on his chocolate face. Everything was in perfect timing. Out came his son, jogging up to the car. His son was so used to their everyday routine, that he didn't pay attention to his surroundings. That's where he fucked up. The sound of screeching tires echoed in the streets. Jazzy ran her car into Mel's car; blocking him in and then the first shot went off ringing through the air of Wisconsin. Instantly, Mel's son hit the ground from a shot to the back of the head. Cornbread let his gun off without thinking twice about it. He then picked the North Face book bag up and threw it on his back. People were screaming and running for their life because they didn't know exactly where the bullets were coming from and they didn't know if they were next.

Up the street, Sharae was getting ready to handle her business. There were only two niggas on the corner this particular day which made it better for her. Only one was strapped. The one who didn't have a gun ran for dear life as soon as he heard the gun go off. The other dude, with his tough ass, shot in the direction of the barbershop, but Sharae was on his ass. Nobody was expecting her pretty ass to be carrying an all-black 9mm with a silencer on it. She gave him a couple of body shots and he went flying to the ground.

Kenya sat in her car and watched everything transpire in front of her. It was like watching a motion picture being filmed right in front of her eyes. Back up the street, Jazzy still had Mel to deal with. He kept his gun on his lap at all times, so it wasn't much for him to let off a couple of shots and he did just that. He let off a couple of rounds as he rammed his car into Jazzy's car, trying to get out of the jam, but that wasn't going to happen. He wasn't going anywhere if it was left up to Cornbread. The shots he fired at Jazzy were lethal. Maybe the Lord did answer her prayer. The bullets went straight past her head, barely missing her and sailing out through the window. She wasn't able to get off any shots because she was too busy ducking from the bullets flying her way. Cornbread had her back though. From the passenger side window, Cornbread reached his arm in the car and gave Mel one shot in the head. Immediately, Mel slumped forward with his head landing on the horn making it go off, but Cornbread didn't stop there. He let off four more slugs in Mel's body. After that, Cornbread scanned the car for the duffle bag quickly. The bag rested on the floor on the passenger side of the car. He reached in the car, grabbed the bag, then ran and hopped in the car with Jazzy. Jazzy was a nervous wreck, as much dirt as she did in these streets, she had never been shot at. She never came that close to death in her life.

"Pull the fuck off!" Cornbread shouted and Jazzy did so without any hesitation. Sharae was running up the streets in their direction and Kenya had met them half way up the block in her vehicle. The cars stopped side by side. Kenya reached her arms out the window while Jazzy tossed her both bags. Kenya screeched off without even a nod of her head. Cruising right behind her was Meech; he gave Cornbread quick eye contact, and then put his focus back on Kenya.

Even though Jazzy was shaken up, she was glad the job was a successful one. The mission was completed without any mishaps. Now it was time they headed back to the hotel, grabbed their things and burned rubber back to the Chi. She was ready to get back home and leave this all behind her. She wanted to forget this day ever happened.

As Cornbread and Jazzy were sitting at a standstill waiting on Sharae to get in the car, gunshots went off. Both Jazzy and Cornbread ducked at the same time while yelling, "Get the fuck in, let's go," to Sharae. Sharae had just put her hand on the back door as more gunshots went off in the streets that they had turned into a crime scene. They didn't see where the shots were coming from.

Jazzy yelled again, "Get the fuck in, let's go!" but it was too late. Sharae never heard those words because her body was taken over by pain. She had been shot in the back. She fell hard against the car then hit the ground. Cornbread got out of the car just blasting. He didn't give a fuck who he hit. He just let off round after round in every direction. After Sharae was shot, the gunshots from the assailant came to a complete halt.

Cornbread got down on the ground next to Sharae and looked at her body. There was no life left inside of her. What really confirmed it was when he gazed into her eyes that were wide opened, her eyes stared back at him, yet there was nothing there. Her soul was gone. There wasn't anything that Cornbread or Jazzy could do.

CHAPTER NINE

Jazzy was in tears as she drove back to the hotel. Her girl, her sister, her ace…was dead and she didn't know who to place the blame on. She wasn't sure if she should blame herself, Vanity, or Ferrari; but no matter who she blamed, Sharae was gone and there was no coming back.

Without giving it a full thought or even thinking twice about it, a motherfucker took Sharae's life. Now Jazzy's heart ached more than ever. She knew something was going to go wrong that day, but she couldn't pinpoint it. Her gut never let her down, and today wasn't any different. As Jazzy continued to shed tears, she felt bad for bringing Sharae into her bullshit. It was her fight and her girl took the ultimate downfall and paid with her life. The more Jazzy thought about Sharae, the more her heart ached, the faster she drove and the tighter she gripped her gun that sat on her lap. She wanted to blast everybody that her eyes landed on. Her heart was so heavy that it felt like an elephant was sitting on it.

"God…why?!" she shouted out. She wasn't looking for a response from Cornbread at all. She wanted God to answer this one for her. She wanted to know why He allowed the devil to interfere. She knew God wasn't going to answer her though, not now anyway, but Cornbread did. He wasn't trying to be mean, but he was keeping it real.

"How could you ask God a dumb ass question like that? Look at us, Jazzy…we out here doing dirt. We do dirt every single day and we just took three people's lives a moment ago. I took two and Sharae took one. So to answer your question, it's simple…if you live by the streets, you will die by the streets and that's exactly what happened to Sharae. That could have been any one of us back there lying breathless. It wasn't our time, it was hers. So pull yourself together; but do know that since Vanity had us out her doing her dirty work, as soon as we get Ferrari back, I'm going to kill Vanity the same way Sharae died –one bullet to the back while running for her life. Or do you want the pleasure?"

"Yeah, I want that bitch all to myself; but that other shit you jaw jacking about, I'm not trying to hear. We didn't kill them boys back there for the fun of it," Jazzy pointed her finger toward the back window. "We are out here on a mission. We not out here killing just because…we out here

116

trying to get my nigga back," she said through tears.

Cornbread didn't have anything else to say, so he just stared ahead in deep thought while Jazzy continue to drive back to the hotel. He thought about Sharae and even though she wasn't his bitch, he was going to miss her. Sharae wasn't supposed to go out like that and he knew it. She had her whole life ahead of her. They all were supposed to make it back to Chicago alive. Nothing was supposed to go wrong. Now Sharae's name carried three horrible letters in front of it: R.I.P. One would never know when it's their time to meet their maker, but Cornbread felt her day came too soon. He understood exactly where Jazzy was coming from, but he was a realist and death will come to us all. Death is funny and it comes without warning. One minute you're here and the next minute you're gone. He really was going to miss her. Just hours ago, she was receiving some good dick from him and now he would never get any of her pussy again. He would never feel the warmth of her walls. He would never get a chance to argue with her again. Everything was over with. No more Sharae.

Cornbread couldn't continue to dwell on what he couldn't change; his main focus at this point was Jazzy. He had to make sure she was alright through this whole ordeal. He noticed how Jazzy was driving. She was driving like a bat out of hell.

"Pull over!" Cornbread shouted to Jazzy. "There's no need for all of us to have R.I.P. in front of our names."

"What?" Jazzy shouted at the top of her lungs not even realizing it.

"Pull the car over Jazzy. Your mind is so far gone that you didn't even realized you just side swiped a car back there. Pull over and I'll drive."

He was right. Jazzy didn't realize what she had just done. Her mind was in another place. A good place where her and her girl were sitting back kicking it and talking shit and Cornbread had fucked all that up when he yelled out, pull over. The tears that fell down her face were coming so heavy that it began to mess with her vision, making it become blurry.

She pulled the car over and her tires kissed the curb. She shifted her car into park and then she yelled out, "This can't be life!" Jazzy's life will forever be different now that her best friend is gone, but her memory will forever live with her.

Again, Cornbread didn't say a word. He just reached over to the driver's seat and his huge manly arms embraced her and she welcomed his touch. His arms felt so good around her that she almost melted in them. She felt his genuine love and she didn't want him to let go. The longer he held her, the more at ease she felt. Cornbread wanted her to know that everything was going to be alright; if nobody else had her, he had her.

* * * * *

Back at the hotel, they packed their things. They pack them as quickly as possible because as soon as they walked into the hotel lobby, there was a flat screen TV mounted on the wall broadcasting the news. They didn't pay it any attention until they heard "Four found dead" and that froze them in their tracks. Everything that they did had flashed right before their eyes at that very moment. If the anchorman didn't have anybody else's attention in that lobby, he had theirs. "Over to you Cheryl," the anchorman said.

The news reporter stood at the edge of the sidewalk with her face made up perfectly and her hair was in the cutest curls. She wore a nice creamed-colored blouse, with a beautiful necklace to bring out her neckline. She had on a navy blue skirt that hugged every curve on her body down to her mid-thigh. She was calling what she saw as something from out of a movie.

She reported, "A young lady was found dead in the street, two young men were found dead on the sidewalk and another man was slumped over in his car. Right now, the police are trying to figure out if this has something to do with the murders that took place on this very same street last week."

Jazzy and Cornbread looked at each other without saying a word, but their eyes spoke for them. They continued to listen as Cheryl talked.

"There was a witness."

Jazzy and Cornbread listened even more closely when they heard the reporter mentioned a witness. Somebody had made them…or did they?

"The police are looking for a dark-colored car with a man and female driver. That was all the information the witness could give, but the police are hard a work trying to figure this one out. They are reviewing surveillance tapes in the area.

Reporting from Channel 2 News, this is Cheryl…back to you, Bob."

Right after that, they took off toward the elevator and Jazzy whispered, "Man and woman in a dark-colored car…that could be anybody. We don't have much to worry about. Shit, more than half of Wisconsin has just been made a murder suspect; but let's get the fuck out of here anyway!"

Cornbread got Sharae's things out of her room because Jazzy couldn't do it, but she knew she had to pull herself together like Cornbread said. She couldn't fall apart…not now anyway, because they still had a major problem, Ferrari was still gone. They finished packing and hit the road. They were on their way back to Chi-town in no time. They road back in silence the same way they drove there, but this silence was different. It was an eerie silence. They felt Sharae's presence in the back seat; Cornbread didn't have a reaction, but Jazzy did. She just smiled, closed her eyes, and thought about the good times she shared with her girl.

* * * * *

"Twenty more minutes and we will be pulling up to your crib," Cornbread said to Jazzy when he saw her blink her eyes open. She had dozed off on the ride home. He wanted to wake her, but she was sleeping so peacefully and now that she was up, he wanted to give her an ear full. "Jazzy, you know I love you; right?" he said never taking his eyes off the road. He sensed the uneasiness that he made her feel when he spoke those three words, but he didn't care. He needed her to understand what he was saying to her and that what he felt was real.

"Here you go with this bullshit again. Please stop, now is not the time," Jazzy said after she popped her lips.

"It will never be the right time if I leave it up to you," he said as gently as possible. He wanted to lash out at her for not wanting or accepting his love. He felt that any woman that he gave his love to should appreciate it and give their love back to him.

"Fuck it, Cornbread…get this shit off your chest if that will make you happy, but make it fast," she said with a jazzy attitude.

"I want to be with you," he said without any hesitation. "I see the shit that Ferrari does and he's not the one for you."

"And you are?" she laughed. "How could you be thinking about a relationship at a time like this anyway? I just lost my best friend and you lost someone you were just fucking hours ago. Oh, you thought I didn't hear you next door; huh?"

"You made me do it. If you weren't being stingy with the pussy, the dick would have been all yours."

Jazzy raised her hand getting ready to smack Cornbread for his smart remark, but she caught herself and he smiled. He knew exactly what he was doing. He was trying to get a reaction out of her and it almost worked, but she knew her place. He wasn't her man, he wasn't worth it, and she knew it. He was free to do whatever he wanted and she didn't have the right to get mad. She shook that little bit of hatred that she had out of her system and relaxed her mind. She sat in silence and waited for him to complete his next thought.

"And yeah, I am the one. You need someone that can be there for you physically, mentally, and spiritually. Ferrari doesn't appreciate a woman like you. He thinks showering a woman with gifts is all there is to a relationship. He doesn't put the time in like he's supposed to, because if he was...I wouldn't be dicking you down three times a week."

Jazzy knew that Cornbread had a point, but she had been around Cornbread for many years, and she knew he was no different than her man. Ferrari spends time with her, but it's not quality time. She didn't put a lot of thought into it because she knew that he was out in the streets taking care of business. Quality time or not, she couldn't be with his friend. She felt twice as bad because she was fucking behind her best friend. She loved Ferrari, and there was nothing that Cornbread could say or do to make her change her mind.

"Do you hear me talking to you, Jazzy?"

"Yeah, I hear you, but…"

"There's no but…I'm not giving up until I have you fully in my life. I'm in love with you," Cornbread said as his eyes glanced back and forth between the road in front of him and at Jazzy's face.

Giggling, Jazzy stated, "None of you niggas know what love is."

"Jazzy, I said my peace and I'm not going to give up."

"Let me ask you this…what about Ferrari? Do you even care how he would feel? What about y'all business arrangements?" she said curiously.

Cornbread contemplated on his next words before he spoke. "He still is going to be my nigga and we are always going to get money together if it's left up to me. I will always have mad love for my nigga, but my happiness is what counts right now. I know he might not accept it. The nigga might even try to kill me for this shit, but I'm willing to take that risk. The love I have for y'all used to be the same…that brotherly and sisterly love; but now the love that I display for y'all is different. I still have brotherly love for him, but as time went on something happened between me and you and I want to keep it that way. And to show you the type of nigga I am…I'm still going to go hard for my homie to get him back home."

Jazzy didn't know what to say behind what Cornbread said. He was speaking some real nigga shit, even though he loves his friend's bitch. Most niggas wouldn't have cared about Ferrari's return, but Cornbread did. He knew how to separate the two. He knew the difference between business and pleasure, and he was determined not to let pussy control his thoughts. He was a real nigga, and they didn't come any realer than Cornbread.

Finally pulling up in front of her crib, all Jazzy wanted to do was lay down and sleep until the next day. So much had happened within a week and she didn't know how much longer it was going to be before she actually broke down. The only person that she could call to air out her dirty laundry to without being judged was Tanya, and before she lay down, she planned to give her a call to tell her all about her week. This is not the way Jazzy had planned for her life to be, but sometimes a woman can get so wrapped up with a lifestyle, that she forgets to actually live.

Jazzy finally got out of the car and so did Cornbread. He grabbed everybody's luggage out the trunk of the car, including Sharae's, and headed to the door. Jazzy walked a couple of feet ahead of him so she could unlock the front door. She stopped at the door, turned around, and looked at Cornbread as he walked toward her. She reached her hands toward the luggage and told Cornbread that she had everything from there, but Cornbread wasn't letting her get away from him that easy. All Jazzy wanted to do was be alone, but Cornbread wasn't about to let that happen.

Upon entering the house, Cornbread put the luggage down and immediately swept her off her feet...literally. As he carried her to her room, he planted a small kiss on her face then undressed her; removing one article of clothing at time. First, he removed her shoes and then he gave her feet a slight massage. His hands made their way up her legs, to her thighs, and then landed on the button of her pants. With one flinch of his thumbs, her pants were unbuttoned. His head dipped toward her silver zipper, and his teeth clinched it, dragging it down as far as it could go. Jazzy lay still without saying a word waiting on him to do what she needed him to do.

His hands made their way to her hips, helping her wiggle her bottom part free. His tongue found what it had been looking for, what it had been craving for –her love box. He gave it three good licks and sucked on her clit making his way up to her stomach. His tongue did circular motions, causing her stomach to cave in and out. Moans escaped her mouth the more he licked. His head then pushed her shirt up to her chest and his hands followed, trimming the upper part of her body. Taking her shirt off, he immediately removed one breast at a time from her bra. Sucking one breast at a time, then both of them at once, it wasn't long before Jazzy was begging for the dick.

"Please…give it to me, Cornbread," she panted and moaned with each word she spoke.

"Give you what, baby?" he asked, even though he knew exactly what she wanted.

"You know what I want, daddy," she said through moans.

"No, I don't. Tell me, baby. Tell daddy what you want," Cornbread said.

"That dick, I want that dick! Now give me my dick right now," she said sexually and it was turning Cornbread on.

His dick had already been at full attention, but he wanted her to know that it was all about her. He wanted to make her feel good before he even gave her the dick. He ended up making love to her for the rest of the day and into the wee hours of the morning like no other man had ever done before. Cornbread was like a poison. He made Jazzy feel weak. He made her go against her words every time she said she was through fuckin' with him. It was going to be hard for her to break away from him. That day, that very moment, he made her forget all about Ferrari and Sharae. He took her pain away. Jazzy didn't have a worry in the world. It was all about her and Cornbread.

CHAPTER TEN

It was 1:15 p.m. when Jazzy woke up. She was full of regrets for the first time in her life after rolling over in her bed and coming face to face with her man's best friend. Cornbread knew she was vulnerable; he was playing off her emotions and now he had Jazzy more confused than ever. If Cornbread hadn't confessed his love to her, she wouldn't be so confused; but Jazzy had to wear her feelings on her sleeves and get focused on getting her man back home. She knew that no matter what Cornbread said to her, there would never be a "them." She could never be with him because her heart belonged to Ferrari.

The guilt was really tearing her up inside so she woke Cornbread up and sent him home. She told him that she would call him later, but she really didn't have any intention on calling him at all. Focused back on the task, Jazzy called Vanity.

"What's up, girly?" Vanity said as she answered the phone.

Jazzy hated the way that Vanity talked to her. Her voice reflections came off as if they were friends and they were far from that.

"My fuckin' friend is dead behind this bullshit. That's what's up!" Jazzy screamed into the phone.

"Why in the hell are you telling me?" Vanity said nonchalantly. "It's not like I had her killed," she then snickered. "You're from the streets, baby girl. You know how shit goes. No matter how you plan something to the T, something can still go wrong, so get over it. You will see her again on the other side; but if you call this phone again screaming in my ear like you crazy, you will see her sooner than you think. Now try me if you want to."

Vanity was a beast with the words. Each word cut Jazzy like a razor and just like a coward, Vanity hung up before Jazzy could throw her sword back at her. Jazzy was pissed and Vanity didn't care how she left her feeling after she hung up. The only thing Vanity cared about was getting money, and nothing else mattered to her. Money was the root of all evil and it had definitely made Vanity an evil bitch.

Jazzy tried calling Ferrari's phone back, but didn't get an answer. She called it again, and again, and still didn't get an answer. Jazzy looked at her phone and tossed it across the room out of frustration. She couldn't believe she let Vanity drive her to the point of almost breaking her phone. At this point, Jazzy's only hope in getting to Vanity before all tasks were complete was through Meech. She was counting on him more than he knew. She was ready to make Vanity feel the pain she was feeling; but until she got the call from Meech, she was going to keep moving forward with the things she had to do to get her man back home.

Jazzy walked through the house in her birthday suit. Her pussy was throbbing with every step she took because Cornbread had beaten the pussy up. He definitely gave her something she could feel. Entering the kitchen, she opened her deep freezer and her hand went right past the fifth of Ciroc and reached deep down in the right corner and grabbed her very last bag of PCP. She walked out of the kitchen, into her living room, and searched her luggage for a blunt. She knew she had one in there because she had planned on smoking on the road, but never got the chance to do it because she had left her bag at home. Making her way over to her couch, her naked ass massaged the leather, while her tongue massaged the blunt with its moisture. She filled it with the content from the bag and sealed the blunt with a kiss.

Before smoking the blunt, Jazzy wanted to look at the picture of the next person she had to take out, which was Toby. She was doing all this for the love of her man and she didn't mind it one bit. Love conquers all. She placed the blunt behind her ear and got right on top of business. She studied Toby's photo for the first time. He actually looked familiar, but she couldn't pinpoint where she knew him from. Toby was a short, fat, light-skinned, preppy-looking dude, with cold black hair and deep dimples. He flashed a gold tooth in one of his pictures. Knowing him or not…he had to go. It was all for the love of Ferrari.

After familiarizing herself with Toby, Jazzy decided she wanted to hit the club because she felt like maybe a change in scenery would change her mood. She needed to get out and enjoy herself despite the bullshit that had been taking place. She picked up the phone to call her girl, Tanya, but hung up before placing the call. She wanted to just pop up over Tanya's house since she hadn't seen her. Jazzy got dressed and headed out the door.

Finally getting a chance to enjoy her blunt, she sat in front of Tanya house and smoked. Tanya hated the smell of PCP and that's why Jazzy stayed in her car to get high. She inhaled and exhaled the toxics as it floated through her blood stream giving her the best high in the world. PCP was a powerful drug, so she knew her limit. She used it, but didn't abuse it. As she continued to puff on her blunt, she closed her eyes as she felt the drug work. Her mind left her body. She was now on Jupiter. This was the highest she had been in a long time and it actually scared her a bit. She opened her eyes and looked at the blunt. She stared at it like she didn't know what it was. She put it out instantly, because she knew if she would have smoked the whole thing, she probably would have been in somebody's psych ward. That drug was that powerful. It was known to many as the Superman high. It would have a motherfucker tripping out. Ferrari used to ask her all the time why she smoke that shit, but she couldn't come up with a legitimate answer. All she ever told him was that it helped her to escape from reality.

Jazzy chilled in front of Tanya's house for about thirty minutes before she got out of the car because she wanted to enjoy her high to the fullest. She knew she had to break the news to Tanya about Sharae, and she didn't want Tanya to blow her high. She knocked on the door a couple of times before Tanya came to the door. For a minute, she thought Tanya wasn't there because she didn't see her car and it took her longer than usual to answer. When she opened the door, Tanya's eyes were swollen and bloodshot red from all the crying she had been doing.

"Where that nigga at," was the first thing Jazzy said to Tanya when she saw her face. She knew that Tanya's boyfriend beat her from time to time, so all fingers pointed to him for the puffy eyes and runny nose. Jazzy had never met him personally. Sharae had already filled her in on the type of nigga he was, and Jazzy felt that there was no need to be in the presence of a man that put his hands on a woman. Jazzy was the type of chick that never got in her friend's business, so she kept her distance.

Sniffling through her words, Tanya said, "What are you talking about? Ain't nobody do nothing to me. I heard about Sharae."

"How in the hell you find that out? That shit happened all the way in Wisconsin."

"The streets always talking…you know that," Tanya stated with a nasty attitude. She didn't have an attitude with Jazzy; she just had an attitude because her girl was gone.

Jazzy had finally made her way through Tanya's door and they both sat on the couch and cried their eyes out. Jazzy really didn't know what to say to comfort Tanya because she was hurting herself. They cried a river in silence until Tanya said, "Do you remember when me, you, and Sharae went to that girl's house and beat her ass for talking shit at the skating rink."

Jazzy didn't have any other choice, but to bust out laughing. It was a moment she would never forget. They sat and reminisce about the good old days, telling story after story. They knew their girl wouldn't want them shedding too many tears over her. They laughed until their stomachs began to hurt. Jazzy really did need that laugh. She had heard that laughter was good for the soul, and she was starting to believe that.

Then Jazzy said, "I think I'm going to take you up on that offer."

"What offer? What are you talking about girl," Tanya asked somewhat puzzled.

"The other day you were trying to get me to go out, I'm all game tonight. We both need to clear our head."

"Sounds like a plan to me. Be ready at 11:00 p.m," Tanya said ready to clear her mind of the hurt she was feeling from missing her girl.

Jazzy said, "Okay." Then got up and left out the door.

* * * * *

Kenya placed her key into the door, turned it, and walked into the crib. Immediately, she felt something wasn't right as soon as she stepped across the threshold. She heard the TV on in her room and she knew damn well that she had turned it off before she had hit the road. Her heels ran across her carpeted floor as she tipped toed through her house. She unzipped the duffel bag and grabbed her gun out of it. Her eyes scanned the large apartment looking for any sign of who could be in her crib, but she found none.

Her house was in a total mess. Clothes were everywhere, but not because someone ransacked it, but because that was the way, she left it. She cared more about her appearance than she cared about the roof over her head. As long as she had furniture, a TV, and food in her crib, she was cool. She didn't have time to be cleaning up. Walking into her bedroom, she saw her brother lying across her bed watching TV. She hadn't had the slightest clue he was there. He normally called before he made an appearance. She wondered why things were different this time.

"Drew, what the fuck are you doing here? And I'm going to get that bitch you fucking fired if she keeps letting you in my crib without my permission. This is her second time doing this. I could be in here walking around butt naked and y'all come through my door."

"We knocked before we entered," he laughed then he got serious. "Are you telling me I can't come and visit my sister?"

"Naw, I'm not saying that and you know it. What happened with a call saying, Sis, I'm on my way…meet me at the crib so I can get in? That's too much like right. You'd rather…for the lack of better words…break in my shit. Keep letting yourself in my crib unexpected, you will find yourself shot. I thought you were an intruder. You see what's in my hand? I was getting ready to riddle your body with bullets," Kenya informed Drew.

Throwing his hands in the air, he laughed, "Alright now, Killa."

She laughed with him. "Fuck you, but you must be in some trouble; that's the only time I see your face around here," Kenya questioned.

"Actually, I am, but it's nothing I can't handle. I just need to lay low for a minute," Drew responded.

"Getting out of town would be considered lying low; not running to your sister's house. I don't want any bullshit coming to my house, Drew. Last time your butt hid out at my crib, they shot that bitch up and I had to pick up and move. I don't want the same thing to happen this time," Kenya with concern in her voice.

"I made sure nobody was following me this time. My bitch put the word out that I'm out of town, so trust me…your house is cool. And check it out…ain't no nigga going to run me out of town; please believe that. I'm not a bitch ass nigga, but I'm not a dumb ass nigga either to stay at my own crib where he could find me," Drew spoke sounding cocky.

"What the fuck you need from me, Drew? You need me to put in some work," Kenya asked.

Even though Kenya and Drew didn't have the best relationship in the world, they were family, and no matter what he needed, she was going to be there for her brother no matter what.

"Nothing major. Just a place to stay for now because I killed a nigga the other day." He didn't let her know it was a shorty. "And I can't stay out west until I get rid of the nigga that is trying to kill me."

"Damn, your trigger happy ass! You need to chill with all that killing shit. How you expect to make money when you out here creating a war? You can't keep letting these niggas pull you off your square like that. Fuck niggas and get money; learn how to control that shit, brah."

"I feel you, sis."

* * * * *

Meech sat outside of Kenya's crib. He got on the phone quickly and called Cornbread to let him know what was up. Kenya had pulled into a nice looking subdivision that was surrounded by lots of trees and a beautiful garden with neatly trimmed grass. There was a nice sized lake that sat in the back of her building that separated the golf course and the actual land she lived on. He watched her closely as she got out her car, never taking his eyes off her as she made her way to her apartment. The apartment she lived in looked like a motel from the outside, so he saw exactly what apartment she went into.

"Boss man," Meech said as soon as he heard Cornbread voice. "The bitch made a stop. I'm not sure if Ferrari is in the crib, but she did get out the car with both bags so this has to be the spot."

"Good job, my nigga, good job. I owe you big time for this," Cornbread said into the phone. "Where you at, I'm on my way. It's time I give them a taste of their own medicine. Do you see any movement going on in the crib?"

"No, I can't see shit from where I'm parked."

"Okay, cool…no worries. Just make sure your eyes stay glued to that door. Let me know if you see anybody else come and go out the apartment. You got your banger with you right?"

"What type of question is that," Meech laughed. "My banger stay glued to my side."

"My type of nigga," Cornbread replied.

It was good timing for Cornbread; he had just jumped in his car leaving Jazzy's crib. Meech gave him the instructions to where he was. He was in a suburb right outside of Chicago and it was only going to take twenty minutes to get there with the speed limit he would be doing. Cornbread felt good about this. He checked for his gun and made sure his clip was full. He was ready to go rescue his homie, kill that bitch Vanity, and whoever else was a part of the kidnapping. Cornbread headed toward the expressway with a smile on his face and with the thought that today was going to be a good day.

"Damn, Cornbread," Meech said, grabbing him from his thoughts.

"Damn what?" Cornbread chatted with concern.

"It's nothing major. I took my eyes off the bitch's crib for a hot second and now she's in her car pulling off."

"Whatever you do, don't let her get out of your sight. I mean that shit, Meech!" Cornbread added more gas to the pedal. He needed to hurry up to check out the spot Kenya had just left while Meech kept a close eye on her.

"Believe me, I'm not. I got this under control…trust me on that one, big homie."

After hanging up the phone with Cornbread, Meech watched as Kenya moved swiftly through traffic while her head moved from side to side as she bounced it to music. The faster she drove, the faster he drove. He was determined not to lose her. He wanted to get closer, but he didn't want to give himself away. There were only two cars that separated the two of them, as they traveled down this road that seem like it was never ending. Kenya busted a right turn after finally coming up to a stop sign and he busted one as well; only leaving one car to separate them now. She drove for about ten more minutes doing thirty miles per hour before she made another right turn. This time he was right on her tail, leaving no cars to separate the two, but not making it noticeable that she was being followed.

Meech turned his music up in the car the loudest it could go. He grabbed his half of a blunt out of the ashtray and placed it between his lips, then lit it. He was in a zone following her as Jay-Z spit his lyrics. He wanted Ferrari back just as bad as anybody else. No, he wasn't Ferrari's right-hand man, but the nigga made sure he kept money in his pocket and that was good enough to have him out in these streets trailing Kenya. Ferrari was a team player, that's what Meech liked most about him. He made sure if he ate, his whole crew ate; and the same was true of Cornbread. They understood

143

there was no "I" in team, and they understood if you treated your crew well, they would treat you better.

Making sure he kept his promise by keeping a close tail on Kenya, Meech became agitated when he looked at his gas hand and noticed the gas light had just popped on. He hoped she hurried up, and find her destination before he ran out of fuel. This bitch has been driving for a long time, Meech thought. Running out of gas would fuck up everything and all his hard work would have been for nothing. Making a left turn, then another left turn, and another one Meech was getting dizzy. It seemed as though they were driving in circles. The thought popped in Meech's head after he saw the blue house to the left of him for the third time, but he blew it off as him being high.

After the last left turn, Kenya cruised up the street and came up on a red light. She sat there for a couple of seconds and they made eye contact when she stared through her review mirror. Then the light turned green, but she didn't move. Meech was wondering why she was at a standstill. He couldn't hear the fire truck coming toward the intersection because his music was just that loud. Kenya knew exactly what she was doing. About five blocks back, is when she realized someone was trailing her. She saw the fire truck getting closer. She smiled at Meech through the mirror and his eyes drifted in another direction. When the fire truck was close enough, but safe for her to precede she took off across the intersection. When she burned rubber, so did Meech, but he didn't make it across successfully. The fire truck ran into the back end of his car knocking him back to the opposite side of the street, up on a curb and into a pole. The car burst into flames instantly. Meech was gone. He was dead just like that, and there wasn't a fire fighter in the world that could save him. Kenya looked through her review mirror again, her lip parted ways cracking a smile and then she went on about her merry little way.

* * * * *

Kenya pulled right into the garage. Vanity smiled when she heard the garage door opened. She knew it was Kenya, the money, and the kilos. She looked at Ferrari and cracked a smile and mouthed the words, mo money, mo money, mo money, mo. He just shook his head. He was so ready for all of this to be over with.

Kenya was upset when she walked into the crib and she wasn't trying to hide it. Anger was written all over her face. She tossed the two bags on the floor and mouthed, "Let's just kill all these motherfuckers and get this over with. Why continue to play this game with them? We have enough money in the bag and enough kilos to set us straight. This shit we just came into is way over $200,000. The profit we are about to make off these kilos alone is more than that."

"Calm down, Kenya. Talk to me, what's wrong?" Vanity said with a puzzled look on her face. She really was wondering why her girl was spazzing out.

"His bitch had a nigga following me," she pointed at Ferrari, "but everything is cool. I took care of that. The nigga is dead and I didn't even have to use my gun. I bet she won't have another motherfucker on my tail."

"So, why are you upset if you took care of the nigga? You acting like the nigga beat your ass and took our shit," Vanity spoke

"It's the fuckin' principle that counts, Vanity. The fuckin' principle!"

"You're right and I'm not even going to argue about that."

146

Vanity got all in Ferrari's face and pointed her finger at his temple. She was so close to him that he smelled her breath. "Your bitch is sneaky I see. I hate a slick bitch. I got her ass," then she put her focus back on Kenya. "Don't worry about it baby. I'm going to handle her myself. I'm going to give her something that she's not even going to see coming."

Dialing up Jazzy's number, she picked up the phone on the first ring. Vanity didn't even give Jazzy a chance to say hello. "Listen here, bitch, that little stunt you called yourself pulling of having Kenya followed didn't work."

"I don't have the slightest clue as to what you are talking about," Jazzy mustered up to say while lying through her teeth.

"So, you want to play stupid; right? Just know the nigga you had following my girl is dead. Any more tricks like that and you can kiss Ferrari goodbye. Let me let you know how serious this shit is. Another move like that, and I'm going to pay your mother a personal visit at 639..."

Jazzy cut her off. "There's no need for that. This is between us. Keep my family out of this. You will have your money, these tasks will be complete, and believe me...no more tricks."

"I hope not. I really hope not and I mean every word I'm saying to you. Play pussy and get fucked if you want to. I don't want to have to kill anybody, but I will. Trust and believe that!"

Just like every other time, Vanity got the last word in and hung up the phone.

Jazzy's heart dropped to her feet after Vanity threw the threat at her about her mother. There were two things she didn't play about: her mother and her man. If she killed her father for her mother, what made Vanity think Jazzy would think twice about putting a slug through her skull? Jazzy's beef with Vanity had become more personal than ever.

Reflecting back on what Vanity had just told her about Meech made her stomach weak. She became nauseous. She bent over and vomited right where she stood. It felt like she was throwing up her insides. She made her way to the bathroom, fell to her knees and continue to regurgitate in the porcelain bowel. Jazzy was a mess. She couldn't understand why this was happening to her. She wondered would she ever see her man again. She made her way back to her room with a dry towel and cleaned up the mess that she had made on her floor. Afterwards, she flopped on her bed and cried her eyes out. The only person that was going to be able to lead her to her man was dead.

CHAPTER ELEVEN

Cornbread had finally made it from the city to the burbs. It took him longer than what he had expected. Even though the expressway was rather crowed, he maneuvered his was through until he came up on Wolf Road. The traffic had come to a complete standstill, so he got off. There was no way he was going to sit in all that traffic. He didn't know if time was on his side, so he needed to hurry up to see who and what was in Kenya's crib that might lead him to his boy if he wasn't in there.

After maneuvering his way on the streets, he finally pulled up to the subdivision and circled through the parking lot checking out the scenery. He knew nothing about the subdivision, so he was checking to see if they had a community patrol cop in the area. He didn't see anyone, so he found a parking space that read visitor on the ground and he parked his car. He was three buildings over from Kenya's crib and he got out of the car and headed toward her apartment. He clearly remembered her apartment number, B12.

Heading up the couple of flights of stairs that lead to Kenya's apartment, Cornbread went right to her door. He put his ear up to it before he made a move. He didn't hear anything. He took that as a good and bad sign. Bad because that meant his boy wasn't in there, and good because he could go through Kenya's stuff and look for clues that might lead him to Ferrari. He reached in his pocket and took out a bobby pin, stuck it in the door and picked the lock. He was a pro at picking locks; that was something he learned in from childhood when he was doing all that breaking and entering. The door was opened in a matter of seconds. When he entered the apartment, it was dark inside except for the light that crept through the mini blinds and the light that was coming from a room where he heard a TV. Then he heard light moans escape from a female's mouth. Cornbread wasn't sure if it was the TV or an actual woman in the room. As he continued to walk in the direction of the room, he kicked a shoe that was in the middle of the floor and it went into the wall.

"Sis, is that you?" Drew shouted from the room. "Don't be mad at me. I didn't know you were coming back so soon. She's putting on her clothes now."

Cornbread just let him talk as he took his place on the side of the bedroom door with his gun in aimed position.

"Sis, do you hear me?" Drew said as he got out of the bed putting on his boxers. "Sis," he called out again, this time coming out of the room. His head met the gun.

"Don't move, motherfucker!"

Drew was pissed. He thought he had been caught slipping again. He thought somebody had followed him to his sister's crib like last time. He was frozen in his steps when he felt the cold barrel against his skull. He thought Meech had found him. He didn't have the slightest clue that Cornbread was there for Kenya instead of him.

Cornbread forced Drew on the couch to take a seat and he motion for the chick to come out of the room. "Yo, bitch, get over here now and don't say a motherfuckin' word."

She hurried out of the room. It was the chick that worked for the subdivision. She came out the room with nothing on but her panties and bra, showing off her flat stomach, big ass, and medium-sized breast. She was a pretty thing that was scared shitless. She was caught at the wrong place at the wrong time.

Cornbread squinted his eyes as they zoomed in closer on Drew; and Drew did the same with his eyes. They both recognized each other, but Cornbread was the first to speak. "You're the same motherfucker that was shooting at me and my homie the other day. Your hoe ass killed his son."

"What the fuck ever nigga, stop with the small talk. I know what I did. There's no need for you to remind me and I know what you are here for. You got me slipping. You got me, so kill me; I'm ready to die," Drew spoke without a fear.

The chick was sitting next to him, crying her eyes out. She didn't sign up for this. She didn't know what to do. This was one day; she wished she had kept her legs closed. All she wanted to do was get out of there and go home; but from the looks of it, the only place she was going was to hell if she didn't pray.

"I'm not letting you off that easy. I'm going to let my homie have the pleasure of killing you. You took away the only thing that mattered to him, so I'm going to give him the enjoyment of taking the only thing that probably matters to you –your life. I'm sure he's going to take his time with you. For every bullet you put in his son, I'm sure he's going to put twice as many bullets in you. I should put a bullet in your ass for shooting at me, but naw, I'll let him handle you," Cornbread laughed devilishly. "I'm here for your sister though. The crazy part is, I didn't even know the bitch was your sister and that I would find you here. I guess you can say I tripped and fell into some shit," he laughed.

With his free hand, Cornbread took his phone out his pocket and called Meech, but he didn't get an answer so he left a voicemail telling him to call him back a.s.a.p. and then he placed his phone back in his pocket.

Cornbread got back on the subject he was there for. "Where the fuck is your sister?" Cornbread asked, never letting his gun leave Meech's head.

"Why in the hell are you looking for my sister?" Drew said seriously. He didn't care that a gun was at his head. He was raised to show no fear. Never let the next man see you sweat is what his pops taught him.

"Just answer the question with your tough ass," Cornbread said as he cocked his gun trying to put fear in Drew, but it didn't work.

Sternly Drew replied, "I don't know."

"Where the fuck is Ferrari," Cornbread asked.

"Ferrari?" Drew said, sounding astonished. "I don't know where the fuck that nigga is. Why in the hell would I know that?"

"I'm going to ask you one more time, and if I don't get the answers I'm looking for, I'm going to shoot you in your right kneecap," he said taking the gun away from Drew's head and tapping him on his knee. He then ordered the chick to go to the refrigerator to get him a potato. She did with no problem. He was going to use the potato as a silencer. He knew he was going to have to put a bullet in Drew's tough ass before Meech got there. Cornbread went back with his questions. "Where is your sister? You know what, scratch that question, where is Ferrari?"

"You keep asking me shit I don't have the answer to, and why are you looking for my sister?"

Boc...

One gunshot went off going right into Drew's kneecap as Cornbread had promised. Drew and the chick screamed at the same time. She screamed as if she had been shot. Drew grabbed his knee and fell back on the couch as blood oozed out.

"You bitch ass nigga!" Drew managed to get out through the pain.

Cornbread didn't say anything because he was too focused on the chick trying to get her irritating ass to be quiet. "Shut the fuck up!" Cornbread yelled out to the chick. She then took her hand and covered her mouth, trying to stop her cries from seeping out.

"You see what you made me do? Now stop with the questions. I'm the only one asking questions around here," Cornbread bit down on his bottom lip because he felt like Drew was trying to play him. "You better get to talking and stop acting like you don't know what's going on."

"I don't. I don't have the slightest clue what you're talking about," Drew said.

Right after that, without thinking twice, Cornbread aimed his gun at the chick and shot her in the chest. Immediately, he aimed the gun back at Drew. "Her blood is on your hands now. Next time, that's going to be you if you don't get to talking."

Laughing through his pain, Drew said, "I barely knew the bitch, so actually, her blood is on your hands, homie," Cornbread was surprised with Drew's choice of words. "Seriously, I don't know shit and even if I did, if I talked or not…you're going to kill me anyway."

Drew was right about one thing, he was going to die regardless. There was no way Cornbread was leaving the house with Drew alive. Cornbread picked up the phone again and called Meech, again the phone went to voicemail. He was really getting the impression that Drew didn't know what he was talking about when it came to Ferrari. He became agitated because he thought as soon as he walked in Kenya's house he was going to find his homie, but that wasn't the case. He was even more agitated that Meech picked a fine time not to answer his phone. He was trying to give him the opportunity to come take the nigga's life that took his son's life.

Gun still aimed at Drew, Cornbread's phone began to ring. Without looking at the caller ID he picked up. He knew it had to be Meech calling him back, but when he heard the sweet voice of Jazzy, his thug mentality changed.

"Not now, Jazzy, I'm right in the middle of something."

"Fuck what you in the middle of…Meech is dead!" Jazzy didn't hold no punch line; she went right for the punch.

Without saying another word, Cornbread's finger put force on the trigger three times and he ran out the door.

Ear still glued to the phone, he heard Jazzy say, "What the fuck was that?" But he didn't answer right away so Jazzy called his name. "Cornbread." Again, he didn't say anything. She cried out, "Cornbread, if you are still there say something."

On that note he said, "I'll tell you all about it. I'll be at your crib shortly."

* * * * *

Calling Cornbread was something that Jazzy didn't want to do. She was going to distance herself from him, but she had to call him to let him know about Meech. Instead of things getting better, it seemed like they were getting worst by the day. She wondered how many more had to die before she found her man.

Through her red eyes, Jazzy looked at her Marilyn Monroe clock that was plastered on the wall. She shook her head as she watched every second tick away. Her palms began to sweat because two hours had already passed and there still was no sign of Cornbread. She hoped he was alright. Even though Cornbread wasn't her man, she would flip out if something horrible happened to him. What weighed somewhat heavy on her mind was the fact that she wanted to know so badly, what had taken place when she was on the phone with him. For a minute, she thought she had lost him when she heard the gunshots. Her heart dropped to her feet because she thought those bullets had actually pierced through Cornbread.

The more she sat there and watched the clock; she began to freak out because ever since Ferrari had been kidnapped, her life had been flipped upside down. Jazzy glanced at her phone to make sure she hadn't missed a call from Cornbread and she hadn't. She just couldn't understand why he hadn't arrived yet. She didn't trust Vanity as far as she could throw her, and she was hoping that she hadn't gotten to Cornbread. Jazzy hoped that he was alright. She seriously couldn't take another death.

Worrying wasn't going to get her anywhere. She finally decided to pick up the phone to call Cornbread, but he didn't answer and that caused her to freak out even more. Her heart rate picked up because it was very unusual for him not to answer; especially a call from her. Finally, she got a text after he missed her call, telling her that he was tied up with some money shit and would be at her in the morning.

She was relieved and that was enough clarity for her. All she wanted to know was that he was alive and he was. After the news she received about Meech, she really didn't feel like going out. She didn't feel like doing anything, but she needed to get out to clear her mind, so she went on ahead and started getting herself ready for the club. She wanted to go and enjoy herself and she planned on doing just that. She laid her all-black mini dress that Ferrari had bought two days before he went missing out on her bed. She went in her closet and grabbed a pair of sparkly red bottoms. There wasn't anything left for her to do besides flatiron her Brazilian 32 inch weave and beat her face with some Christian Dior makeup. Jazzy texted Tanya's phone and told her that instead of Tanya picking her up, she would meet her at her crib.

CHAPTER TWELVE

Ferrari sat in the living room and watched Vanity count out the money as Kenya split up the kilos they had just come into. Money signs were in his eyes as he stared ahead at them. There was twelve kilos stacked in piles of four on the table. Vanity had rubber band stacks of money together every time she counted to $1,000. These bitches were money hungry. How did he get mixed up with them two, he questioned himself. These bitches were dangerous, and they wouldn't stop until they got what they wanted. They both were married to Ben Franklin and nobody or nothing was going to come between them from getting that money. What wouldn't they do for the love of money, he thought.

Vanity saw the way Ferrari was staring at them as they got the shit in order. He watched them from a distance as he sat in a wood chair. Vanity walked over to him with a mini skirt on and a pair of stilettoes that showed off her legs, giving her an extra four inches in height. She circled him, while her hand rubbed on his chest like she was about to give him a lap dance. She licked her lips, and then she licked the side of his face, "I like you," she said, "but I hate your bitch and once all of this is over with, I'm going to kill her; so I hope you can live without her."

Ferrari knew that Vanity was the type of chick that liked to be in control. She wanted to feel dominate and he let her feel that power. "Do what you want. If that would make you feel good,"

He didn't feel like going back and forth with her despite the situation at hand. He just wanted Jazzy to complete those tasks and then things would go back to normal. He wasn't trying to hear that garbage Vanity was talking. He was not going to let her kill Jazzy if that was the last thing that he did. The only killing that would be happening would be with him pulling the trigger.

Clearing her throat, Kenya interrupted their conversation because she knew that Vanity had a thing for Ferrari, but Kenya wasn't having it. Vanity was her bitch; and if she kept disrespecting Kenya in her face, she was going to put a bullet through both of their asses. Kenya always took the back seat when it came to Vanity because she took care of her. Kenya loved the shit out of Vanity and she wasn't going to let no dick come in between that.

Vanity and Kenya met when they were in jail. Vanity had taken a liking to Kenya instantly because she liked her style. She was laid back and to herself which was Vanity's speed. She hated a flamboyant chick. Most bitches in jail knew of Vanity because of the stories they heard about her father, so they flocked to her. He was a legend to many. He supplied all of the Philippines and most high-traffic cities in the U.S. Kenya knew nothing about Vanity's father, so Vanity felt the love that Kenya displayed was genuine.

Kenya and Vanity were lovers for about a year before Vanity was released from prison. Vanity was in the joint for real estate fraud. The shit she did, she didn't have to do because she could have gotten anything she wanted out of her father, but having money just given to her without her working for it, wasn't a challenge. It made her life boring, so she went out looking for excitement and her excitement landed her in jail on many occasions. She knew how to do all the illegal hustles. She was a jack-of-all-trades.

Finding love in jail was something the Vanity thought would never happen. She loved Kenya for a whole year and made her a promise before she was released. She promised Kenya that

163

she would hold her down for the remaining of the two years she had, and when Kenya came home, be prepared to live life like a boss bitch. Indeed, when Kenya was released, Vanity kept her promise to her. She came home to a fully furnished crib and a brand new car. Kenya didn't understand why they weren't living together. Vanity was against the whole live-in situation. Vanity needed her space, but Kenya couldn't understand why if they were lovers. After a while, it didn't bother Kenya anymore about not moving in with Vanity. She felt as long as Vanity lived up to her promise; she was good.

After a few months of being free in the world, Kenya began to learn Vanity's character was controlling, and that was the only thing that Kenya didn't like about her. Vanity wanted things done when she said it. It was always her way, nobody else's way mattered. Kenya thought about leaving Vanity on multiple occasions, but she stuck it out because even though Vanity was controlling, she showed Kenya much love. They were lovers and partners in crime; and there wasn't anything in this world that Kenya wouldn't do for her bitch.

* * * * *

Kenya had gotten her cut from the
Wisconsin sting. It was now time she headed
home. She wanted to stay there with Ferrari and
Vanity a while longer, but she trusted her bitch to a
degree. Kenya hoped that Vanity wouldn't jump
on Ferrari's dick and give him a ride of his life, but
if she ever found out that she did, it would be
murder she wrote. Kenya walked over to Vanity as
Ferrari stared on. She palmed her fat ass and stuck
her tongue down her throat. She marked her
property and she wanted Ferrari to know that
Vanity was hers and that he was only there for one
reason and one reason only.

Before pulling out of the garage, Kenya took
out her phone to call her brother. She didn't want
to walk in her crib and he was in there doing God's
knows what. Of course, he didn't answer, so she
text his phone to let him know she was on her way.
Her text simply stated, 'clear all the hoes out my
house, I'm on my way.'

About fifteen minutes into Kenya's drive, it
had started to rain. She hated the rain and it had
begun to come down heavy. Thundering and
lighting had come into effect and she couldn't wait

until she got home. They say when it rained it meant God was crying and she wondered what had Him shedding so many tears of anger, but she would soon find out. Finally pulling up to her subdivision, Kenya noticed that it was a black out. The rain had knocked out all the power. It was pitch black; all she saw through people's windows were small candles burning, serving as their source of light. There was no way she was going to stay there with no lights. She called Vanity's phone and told her that she was coming back to spend the night because she had no electricity and there was no telling when the lights would be back on. Vanity didn't object. At this point, all Kenya wanted to do was make sure her brother was straight.

Kenya reached over to the back seat and reach on the floor by the passenger side. She had a small bag full of money sitting inside a large bag with her kilos in it. She tossed her money bag to the side. She was taking that back to Vanity's with her. She loved her brother, but she didn't trust him to have that large of an amount of money lying around him. He was going to work for his money if he wanted it. She was going to give him the kilos and split the profit with him. That was normally how things have been going anyway.

She grabbed the bag full of kilos, along with her small Gucci handbag, and looked around in the darkness as she ran toward her crib. She skipped the stairs, two at a time, trying to get out of the rain; but she almost tripped when she got to the fourth step. She kicked a toy truck that was sitting on the stairs. She made a mental note to go to her neighbor's crib to tell them about their kid's toys being left on the stairs.

Wet, but not soaked, Kenya flipped through her key ring until she came upon the right key to her door while she walked along the rails to her apartment. Standing in front of her door, she sensed something wasn't right because her door was cracked opened. She called out her brother's name before she entered, but there wasn't any answer. She checked her surroundings before she walked into her crib, because it felt like there were a set of eyes on her. Upon entering into the crib, she moved cautiously as she called out Drew's name again, still no answer. She then used her cell phone for light. The phone lit the crib just enough for her to see two dead bodies on her couch. Kenya didn't scream at all. She knew her brother would be meeting his maker soon. She simply walked over to her brother's bloody body and embraced him while using two fingers to close his eyes.

"Are you alright," asked Bo. Bo was one of her neighbors and the set of eyes that she felt on her were his. She didn't answer. She just sat on the couch rocking her brother back and forth, like she was putting him to sleep, so Bo spoke again. "I saw who did this."

She looked up at him because he now had her undivided attention. Bo went on to tell her that he saw a man emerge from her apartment and he left the door wide opened. He knew something wasn't right, so he went to her apartment and discovered the two bodies. He was going to call the police, but he knew the type of chick Kenya was. He knew she would have wanted to see her brother's body before the corners came and whisked him away. Then Bo told her it was a big nigga and he described Cornbread right to the T.

Kenya knew exactly who was behind this once Bo finished with his description. She looked at Bo and said, "Call the police so they can come and clean this shit up. I have some business to handle."

Kenya ran back to her car in the rain, she now knew why God was so angry. She picked up the phone and called Vanity to let her know what had happened. She told her that there was a change in plans. Cornbread was all hers and she was going to be the one that put him out of his misery.

CHAPTER THIRTEEN

"The time is now or never. These motherfuckers have to go," Jazzy thought as she reminisced over the things she knew she had to do while she polished her gun to give it the perfect shine. She had that baby almost shining like a Jacob – the jeweler diamond. She was getting her chromed out .22 ready for a battle that the next motherfucker didn't even see coming. After she was able to see her reflection on her gun, she placed it down on the living room table, picked up her clip, and loaded it with bullets one by one, giving the last bullet the kiss of death. Death was right around the corner for somebody and soon, somebody's parents would be crying their hearts and souls out. Jazzy didn't want to have nobody's blood on her hands or her conscience, but she knew what had to be done. She closed her eyes and started to say a prayer, but she quickly opened them back up.

"Fuck a prayer!" she shouted as the words rolled off her intoxicated tongue. She was upset because the last time she said a prayer, God didn't answer it and He allowed the devil to interfere.

Jazzy took a sip of her peach Ciroc that sat on the side of her to calm her nerves a little, and then she got off the couch and headed to the kitchen. Neatly spread out on the kitchen table, were the pictures of her last two marks. She stared at both men. She wondered what they could have done to Vanity to make her want to take their life, but none of that really mattered to her. The only person's life that mattered, at this point, was Ferrari's.

Going back and forth between each guy's picture, Jazzy pointed her index finger and then she began to sing, "Eeny meeny miny, moe…which one of you motherfuckers will be the first to go," she smiled as her finger landed on her next victim, but her heart saddened. She shook that feeling fast because there wasn't any time for a pity party. Her saddened heart instantly turned cold. It was do or die time. If she didn't do…then Ferrari would definitely die. The clock was steadily ticking, and the days were flying by faster than she thought. After staring at her target picture for what seemed like an hour, Jazzy walked back in her living room, stood in front of her fireplace and stared at the painting above it. It was a picture of her and Ferrari. She blew the picture a kiss and spoke the words, "I love you. You will be home soon."

Jazzy then pranced over to the table where her gun lie and she picked it up and loaded the clip into it. She then placed her gun in the waistline of her jeans and her Victoria Secret panties, grabbed her jacket and headed out the door.

Cruising through the Westside of Chicago, Jazzy drove to where her target would be. He hung out at a clubhouse called, Dynasty's. She pulled right up to the front door and grabbed a park because she wanted to spot her target before he made his way through. As she cracked on her ranch sunflower seeds, she thought about shooting him from the back as he walked passed her car, giving him a quick and unexpected death; but that would be a cowardly move. She wanted to get up close and personal. She wanted to know the ties between him and Vanity.

Sitting under tint in Tanya's car, Jazzy waited tolerantly. When the sign on the window lit up like a Christmas tree that was her cue that it was almost time for the clubhouse to open for the many carloads of people that were pulling up. People were getting ready to enjoy themselves, while Jazzy was getting ready to take somebody's life. As Jazzy continued to wait on her target to arrive, her phone began to ring. She looked at her phone and it was Cornbread calling. She immediately sent him to voicemail. She didn't want to hear his voice because it would serve as a distraction.

As the streets began to fill up with more cars and motorcycles, Jazzy's eyes drifted to everyone in hopes that her target would be pulling up soon. She wasn't moving out of that spot until she saw the person that she came there for. Moments later, she saw him appear out of nowhere. She didn't see what car he got out of. All she saw was him strolling across the street with some light-skinned chick on his arm. They stood outside the club and talked for a minute, then headed inside and Jazzy wasn't too far behind. She got out the car, dressed for the occasion; all black everything. For some reason, black was the chosen color whenever it was time to lay somebody to rest. Black symbolizes mourning and after she does what she came to do, there would be plenty of motherfuckers mourning over him.

Jazzy's hips swayed from side to side, as she walked to the front door. Her weave hung to the center of her back as it blew with the wind. She took a deep breath, savoring all the good air before she walked through the heavy glass door. Upon entering, she bobbed her head to the music, but was stopped in her tracks as she tried to walk right passed the security guard.

"Are you a member, pretty lady?" the club security guard asked as he undressed her with his eyes. He knew under those clothes was a flawless body, and if she gave him the time of day, he would be all in those guts.

"No, I'm not a member," she said with a calm attitude, but she tried to walk past him again and off course, she didn't get past him. The bald head, slim security guard grabbed her arm this time, which caused her to flare up a little; but she calmed down quickly, because she was there for one reason and one reason only. She knew he was a new security guard; that was another reason why she calmed down.

"Just because you're pretty doesn't mean that you will be getting in here free…, five dollars please," he said seriously.

Jazzy snatched her arm away from him and looked at him like a fool for insulting her character. "No, I'm not expecting to get in off my pretty looks. But since my man is part owner of this spot, that means I get in free." She didn't wait for him to respond she just forced her way past him this time.

The crowd had formed quickly and her eyes zoomed around the room looking for her target. She spotted him over in the corner tucked away with the same light-skinned girl he came in the club with. They were giggling, hugging, and kissing; and Jazzy was going to let him have his last fun because after that…straight to hell he goes.

Jazzy sat at the bar, which was a couple of feet from the door, and she turned her back on her target so he wouldn't suspect her of watching him. As long as she had her eye on the door, he wouldn't be leaving out without her knowing.

From the corner of her left eye, she was still able to see them do what lovebirds do. Jazzy became jealous because that could have been her and Ferrari being lovey dovey; but now she's in the streets on some gangsta shit. The things women do for the ones they love, she thought. Ferrari was her weakness and Vanity knew that, but sooner than later Vanity will see just how hard, she really rode for her nigga.

Hypnotized by the music, Jazzy sipped on a strawberry daiquiri and she enjoyed it as she slurped it through her straw. She didn't want to drink anything hard to add to what she already had earlier because she would have been off her square. Being drunk isn't a good look when she was out trying to handle some business. She needed to have a clear mind so she could kill exactly who she was there to kill...not innocent bystanders.

"Hey, that's my song," Jazzy stated to herself. She snapped her fingers, bobbed her head to the beat, and closed her eyes while letting the music take over her body. The DJ was jamming. He played her and Ferrari's favorite song. In the process of her eyes being closed, Jazzy felt a pair of hands touch her shoulder. She opened her eyes and shook her head before she turned around. She was pissed that somebody had fucked up her zone. She knew plenty of people in the club because of Ferrari, but most would just speak and keep it moving, not stop to hold a conversation with her, so she wondered who could be fuckin' with her zone. When she turned around, her eyes landed on Cornbread and her eyes bulked a little.

"What up, Jazzy?" he said loudly over the music. "Sorry I didn't stop by your crib like I told you I would. I've been out in the streets trying to get that money together so my dude can be returned safely."

"No worries," Jazzy stated nonchalantly. She didn't need Cornbread in her ear right now because he was starting to fuck up her vibe.

"What are you doing in here? You never come in this spot," Cornbread inquired.

"I just needed some air. I wanted to be around people that thought highly of and respected my man. Is something wrong with that?" Jazzy said with a nasty attitude.

"What's with the attitude, Jazzy," Cornbread asked puzzled. "You're acting like a pit bull in a skirt right now that's ready to get loose. Calm down. I'm not the enemy; remember we are on the same team."

"My fault, Cornbread, I just have a lot on my mind. This shit isn't right," she stated and shook her head. All type of things started to go through Jazzy's head. She repeated it again, "This shit isn't right."

"I know you missing Ferrari. Let me do what I do best and help you take your mind off of him," Cornbread conversed as he blew on the back of her neck. Nobody was paying them any attention. He got away with what he knew he could get away with. He would never put Jazzy in an uncomfortable position in public.

"Cornbread...not here," she said as she looked him in his eyes.

"Why not here? You're stressing now, at this very moment; let me help take away some of the pain that you are feeling. Nobody will expect anything. They know you are Ferrari's girl and I'm his right-hand man; and when we go in the back to my office, they will think we are in there on business."

"Are you sure," Jazzy asked.

"Yes, I'm sure. Why do you seem so tense? Just relax, baby."

Jazzy did just that. She relaxed as she took a couple of deep breaths.

Cornbread walked off and so did Jazzy; following his lead. If looks could kill, she would be a dead woman. The light-skinned chick that she saw cuddled up in the corner, stared at her with vengeance in her eyes.

As soon as Jazzy stepped into the office, Cornbread pushed her back against the wall and cupped her breast in his hand, inviting it to his mouth. He was rough with Jazzy. He had some built-up loving making that he wanted to release.

Their lips meet; slopping each other down as their tongues intertwined with each other. Jazzy's lips left his as they made their way to his neck. Her hands fumbled to his belt, to his button, and then to his zipper. His oversized pants immediately dropped to his ankles. Jazzy got on her knees and slopped on his nob. She gave him five good minutes of the best head he had ever come in contact with. Jazzy made her way back up to his lips and planted more kissing on them. She eased her gun from around her back as she continued to kiss Cornbread. He felt a cold barrel on his head and that's when the kissing stopped.

She looked him dead in his eyes, "Cornbread, I love you, but I love my man more..."

Part 2 Coming Soon...

HOW FAR WILL YOU *RIDE*
FOR YOUR NIGGA?

Riding Dirty 2

SHONEY K

Check out these other great reads by author Shoney K

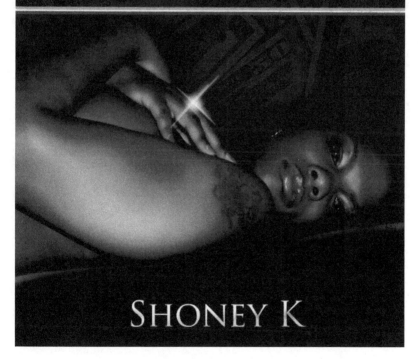

HUSTLE2HARD PUBLICATIONS PRESENTS

FOR THE LOVE OF
MONEY

A NOVEL

SHONEY K

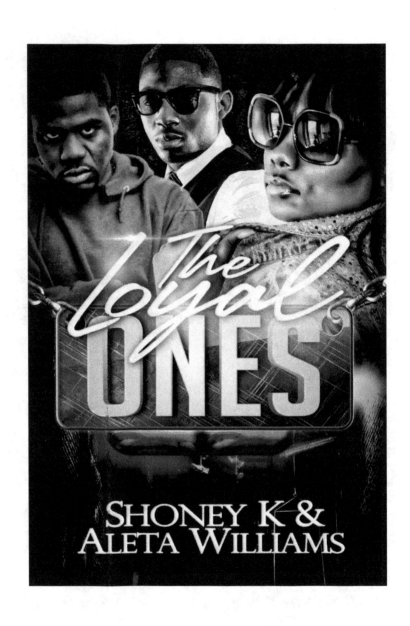

CPSIA information can be obtained
at www.ICGtesting.com
Printed in the USA
LVHW050820130120
643361LV00016B/1107/P